Clint Dennison—He's sworn to do whatever he must to save his father's ranch, and he's got the guns and the guts to back his play.

Helen Bromfield—Despite her almost paralyzing fear and disgust, she would challenge her kidnappers in a most daring way.

Sheriff Rex Barney—A veteran of too many bloody trails, he still never expected a solo bank robbery to lead him to a treacherous explosion of violence and danger.

Lorna May—With a small, almost doll-like face and figure, she is not much more than a girl yet well on her way to becoming a hard, deadly woman.

The Stagecoach Series
Ask your bookseller for the books you have missed

STAGECOACH STATION 14:

CIMARRON

Hank Mitchum

 Created by the producers of
Wagons West, White Indian,
and **Saga of the Southwest.**

Chairman of the Board: Lyle Kenyon Engel

BANTAM BOOKS

TORONTO • NEW YORK • LONDON • SYDNEY • AUCKLAND

STAGECOACH STATION 14: CIMARRON

A Bantam Book / October 1984

Produced by Book Creations, Inc.
Chairman of the Board: Lyle Kenyon Engel

ISBN 0-553-24442-6

Published simultaneously in the United States and Canada

*Bantam Books are published by Bantam Books, Inc. Its trade-
mark, consisting of the words "Bantam Books" and the portrayal
of a rooster, is Registered in U.S. Patent and Trademark Office
and in other countries. Marca Registrada. Bantam Books, Inc.,
666 Fifth Avenue, New York, New York 10103.*

PRINTED IN THE UNITED STATES OF AMERICA

O   0 9 8 7 6 5 4 3 2 1

STAGECOACH STATION 14:

CIMARRON

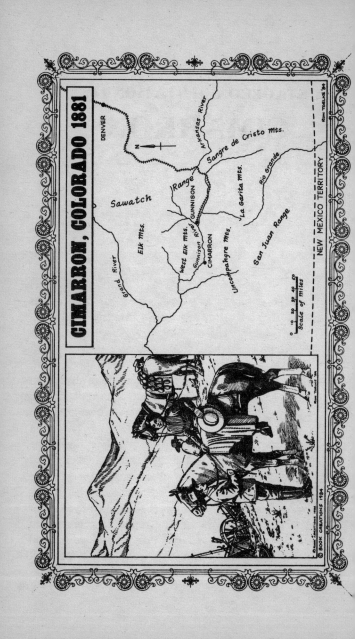

Chapter One

Helen Bromfield was on her way back into the hotel when she noticed the increased activity in front of the Rocky Mountain Express and Stage Company. Four men, obviously straining to their utmost, were pulling the repaired stagecoach from the carriage shed.

Was the long delay finally at an end? It appeared so, but she did not know whether to be pleased or dismayed. So far, her journey in August 1881 across the continent to Gunnison, Colorado Territory, had been accomplished in the comparative comfort of a train. But she had spent enough hours in a Concord coach on other occasions to be fully aware of the swaying ride and dusty trail that awaited her on the final leg of her trip to Cimarron.

Tall, almost commanding in presence, Helen Bromfield was a handsome woman with sharp blue eyes under wide, arching brows. Unconsciously she had compressed her full lips into a prim, straight line, an attitude she had assumed in order to discourage the many men in the hotel who had already noticed her. She was wearing a bottle-green dress with a stylishly tight waist and skirts that lightly brushed the patent leather of her high-button shoes. Her thick, auburn curls were swept decorously up under her straw boater.

As Helen started once again for the hotel lobby, John Ferris, a passenger who had taken the same train from Denver, emerged from the hotel.

"Well, well," he remarked, pausing beside her. "They have finished repairing the coach, have they?"

Helen nodded and looked back at the express office as the stage halted in front of it. "Yes, I believe so," she replied coldly.

She knew Ferris was an actor. She was doing her best to be civil to him, but she did not approve of either the man or his profession.

Ferris glanced at her, undiscouraged. "Well, then, you must allow me to help you with your luggage when the time comes to load up," he said.

"Thank you," she replied icily. "You are very kind."

He inclined his head slightly, the trace of an ironic smile on his pale face. "My pleasure, ma'am."

"But are you sure you can handle my trunks, Mr. Ferris? They are really quite heavy."

His laugh mocked the concern she obviously did not feel. "I assure you, Miss Bromfield, I would not attempt such a Herculean feat alone. I intend to enlist the aid of the bellboy and the desk clerk. Together, I am sure we will manage."

He coughed softly and strode past her, dismissing her most effectively.

The ease with which he dismissed her infuriated Helen. But she convinced herself the man was not worth bothering with, and she headed for the hotel door.

As Helen vanished into the hotel, John Ferris glanced back at her, an amused gleam in his eye. He knew Helen Bromfield for what she was—a haughty bluenose from Boston. Her Puritan background had evidently succeeded in drawing all the blood from her veins. Though he was certain there must be a heart beneath that prim blouse of hers, it probably throbbed with the bloodless, mechanical passion of a toy drummer. *Too bad,* he thought. *She is a most handsome woman.*

But such matters need not concern him anymore. He was past worrying about such foolishness. All that was behind him.

Turning, he idly watched the continued burst of activity in front of the express office. As he stood on the hotel porch, the people passing by along the main street of Gunnison were unable to ignore his dashing, even flamboyant figure. From Ferris's shoulders hung a long, flowing cape lined with red satin. In keeping with the fashion of the times, his dark trousers were sculpted to follow closely the contours of his slim legs. High-button shoes with faun-colored spats encased his feet, and his thick, raven hair was topped by a jaunty, thin-brimmed hat, a small red feather stuck in its band.

In the midst of the raw, dusty railhead town of Gunnison, high in the Rockies, John Ferris was a rare and exotic bird, indeed.

Across the street, a few buildings down from the express office, Annie Foster came out of Ivar Peterson's General Store. In her late twenties, the widow was a tall, spare, bony woman, whose beauty lay in the warmth of her expressive eyes and in the calm, almost serene cast to her plain features.

The clerk helped load her flatbed wagon. Her son,

Ephraim, a towheaded boy of ten, was nearly hidden under a sack of flour the clerk had draped over his small shoulders. As Annie lifted her six-year-old daughter, Marylou, up onto the wagon seat, she happened to glance across the street at the striking figure standing on the hotel porch.

Smiling to herself, Annie recognized the man for an actor. As a young girl in Philadelphia, she often had accompanied her parents to the theater, and this actor looked as if he were about to launch into a scene from *Hamlet*.

What on earth is he doing in this isolated town? Annie wondered. But she thought no more about it as she thanked the clerk for his help and gave young Ephraim a hand lifting the flour sack into their wagon.

"Thanks, Ma," Ephraim said, puffing. "Guess you were right. It was a mite heavy, at that."

"You did fine, son," she told him. "I'm sure the clerk appreciated your help. Now, tell me. Would you like to drive the team?"

Ephraim's eyes widened in delight. "Sure, Ma!"

Smiling, Annie moved aside as the boy scrambled up onto the seat beside her. Lifting Marylou gently, she placed the girl between herself and Ephraim. The young lad carefully adjusted the reins in his small hands and then slapped them across the horses' backs, shouting imperiously, "Gee up!"

The horses started eagerly, and with Annie watching carefully, Ephraim executed a neat full turn. Then, urging the team to a smart gallop, Ephraim drove the team past the waiting stage in front of the express office and headed out of town.

Annie leaned back in her seat proudly. As she passed

townspeople she recognized, she waved to them. They waved back, grinning.

"How'm I doin', Ma?" Ephraim asked, the reins held high, his eyes glowing.

"Just fine," Annie replied. "Keep the team moving along now. Don't let them hang back. The Cimarron stage looks like it might be moving out soon, and I want to keep well ahead of it. Otherwise, we'll be eating its dust."

"Don't you worry, Ma!" Ephraim proclaimed. "We'll stay ahead."

Annie squeezed Marylou, delighted at the way Ephraim was handling the team. She realized he would tire soon. But it was such a comfort to have someone else drive for a while.

Marylou snuggled close to her mother and looked up at her. "Mother?"

"Yes, Marylou?"

"When I get bigger, can I drive the wagon, too?" the girl asked.

"Of course!"

"Next week?" Marylou's face glowed with excitement at the prospect.

Annie laughed and squeezed her daughter still tighter. "We'll see," she promised. "We'll see."

As Ephraim drove down the street, the stage driver, Bruce MacDougal, strode out onto the express office porch. MacDougal was a husky, leathery-faced man in his late forties, with the stub of a cigar stuck in his bulldog mouth. His body was meaty in the shoulders and forearms, and his thick waist was as solid as a tree trunk. Having begun his career years before as a shotgun rider for the famed California Stage Company, MacDougal was recognized as the best driver on the Rocky Mountain line.

Watching young Ephraim driving the team for his mother, MacDougal smiled. The youngster was doing just fine. MacDougal knew Annie Foster only slightly, but like everyone else in Gunnison, he admired her courage, living alone so far beyond the badlands with only her two kids and no man beside her.

As the flatbed wagon disappeared from sight, MacDougal took an appreciative look at the six powerful horses the wrangler was backing into the stagecoach's traces. Then he turned to the express clerk, who was coming out of the express office.

"You're right, Slim," MacDougal commented. "Those are fine-looking horses."

"Like I told you, I've been saving them for this shipment," the clerk said. "They're the best in my stable."

MacDougal looked back at the handsome Percheron brutes as they stamped and shook their heads in anticipation of the hard pull ahead of them. "It's not the horses I'm worried about. It's Carl Sutter."

"No reason for you to worry about him. He's just a hothead who thinks he should be a driver," Slim said.

"There's more to him than that," MacDougal insisted. "And I still think that was him hanging around the carriage shed last night."

The clerk shook his head wearily. "I'm telling you, Bruce, it's the horses you should be worrying about, not Carl Sutter."

"I hope you're right." MacDougal turned and started back into the express office. "But just in case, I'll go get Billy and make sure he's got that shotgun of his oiled and ready for action."

"How soon can you pull out?" Slim asked.

"Give me half an hour."

"Good."

"How many passengers we got for Cimarron?" MacDougal asked.

"Them two that came in on the train and two more," Slim said.

"Two more?" MacDougal was surprised.

Slim nodded unhappily. "And I must admit, I don't like the looks of either one of them. But they had the money, so I had to give them tickets."

MacDougal frowned. "All right, Billy and I will keep an eye on them. But that's all—no more passengers, Slim. Don't let anyone else buy a ticket. I don't care what excuse you give. We've got enough of a load as it is."

"Do you want me to cancel them last two tickets I sold? I can do it if you want," the clerk told the driver.

"No. That'd only cause a stir. We don't want to draw any more attention to this run than we have already."

MacDougal disappeared inside the express office, while Slim continued down the steps to speak to the wrangler.

The Palace Saloon was a block away from the Rocky Mountain Express and Stage Company office. It was not the finest saloon in Gunnison, but at the moment it was the quietest. At a table against the back wall, Carl Sutter was conferring softly with the two new passengers for the stagecoach.

Sutter was a rangy young man with eyes that burned with an eager, almost feverish light. He was not very clean, and his gaunt face was unshaven. He had long, stringy yellow hair that hung down in untidy clots on his shoulders. As he spoke, he leaned close to his two partners.

"I got to ride out now, so you two get ready. Keep low until I'm gone. And when you get on that stage, be nice to that sonofabitch MacDougal. And Billy, too. Don't cause any stir until I show up. You got that?''

"We got it. We got it," said Sam Dodge. "You don't need to keep tellin' us."

"That's for me to decide, Sam. You questionin' my scheme?"

"Hell no, Carl," Dodge said, pulling back from Sutter's mean gaze. Dodge had a huge belly, and his small pig eyes were stuck like tiny raisins in his doughy face. "I just mean you been over this enough."

Sutter sat back in his seat and regarded Dodge intently. "Just so it goes smooth. There ain't no harm in that, is there?"

"No, there ain't, Carl," broke in the other passenger, a tough-looking young woman in her early twenties. Because of her small-boned features, Lorna May looked even younger than she was. Long, reddish curls reached past her shoulders, and her lips were small but full. Her hazel eyes had a cold, calculating light in them.

"Sam's right," Lorna May said. "We been over this enough. I'm gettin' sick of it, myself. The only thing I'm worried about is whether that gold is where you think it is. You didn't get much of a look last night."

"It's there, I tell you!" Sutter insisted.

"Okay," Lorna said. "Okay. It's there. I believe you."

"Yeah," Sam Dodge said eagerly, "I believe you too, Carl. It's there, and we're goin' to get it."

Sutter got to his feet and slapped his black, floppy-brimmed hat down onto his head. Now that the time for action had finally come, he could feel the excitement transforming him, filling him with eagerness. He was wearing a checked cotton shirt, black vest, Levi's, and a pair of very fancy boots. Around his narrow waist hung a pearl-handled Colt in addition to a huge bowie knife. In his right hand he carried a Winchester rifle chambered for the same caliber as his Colt.

"Guess I'll pull out right now," he said.

Dodge and Lorna May nodded.

With a quick glance around the nearly empty saloon, Sutter disappeared through the rear door. A moment later his two friends heard Sutter's horse galloping down the alley. Both Dodge and Lorna May were obviously relieved Sutter had gone. Dodge licked his lips and glanced at the young woman. He was about to smile at her when he saw the cold, hands-off gleam in her eyes and thought better of it.

"I'm ready for a beer," Dodge told her, hauling his bulky figure out of his chair and heading for the bar.

"Get me one, too," Lorna May told him.

It was more a command than a request.

Meanwhile, inside Gunnison's only bank—the Miner's and Cattleman's Savings and Loan—Merlin Oppenheimer heard someone open and then close the rear door. Looking up from his ledger, he watched as a tall man he did not recognize halted in the doorway to Oppenheimer's private office. The stranger was over six feet tall and was wearing a black, flat-crowned Stetson. A dusty saddlebag was draped over one shoulder. Frowning, Oppenheimer put his pen down and got to his feet, then noticed with some trepidation that the stranger was wearing a gunbelt.

The bank president was a slender man with thin strands of black hair combed straight back over his narrow skull and held in place with macassar oil. His eyes were pale blue and peered at the stranger through steel-rimmed spectacles.

"I am sorry, sir," Oppenheimer said, clearing his throat nervously, "but the bank is closed today."

The tall fellow nodded pleasantly enough. "I figured it would be. Not too many banks are open on a Saturday afternoon."

"Then I suggest you come back Monday."

"I can't do that," the stranger said.

"I don't understand." Oppenheimer rubbed his hands together nervously.

"I can't wait until Monday. I need a loan now," the stranger insisted quietly.

"Well, I am sorry," Oppenheimer said decisively. "You will simply have to return during banking hours and fill out an application."

In an attempt to finish with the matter, Oppenheimer sat down and reached for his pen. But the stranger did not leave. Still smiling pleasantly, he strode into the office and took a seat. Then, doffing his hat politely, he placed it carefully on the edge of Oppenheimer's desk.

"I guess you'd be the bank president," he said.

"You are quite right," Oppenheimer replied. "But I fail to see what difference that makes."

"Oh, it makes a difference, all right. If you're the president, you're the gent who has to approve my loan," the stranger pointed out.

Oppenheimer sighed with irritation. "I do not see why you persist in misunderstanding me, sir. I cannot grant you a loan today, even assuming your credentials are in order and you have the required collateral. As I have already explained and do not wish to explain again, this bank is closed."

"Well, yes, I suppose it is. But the thing is, I prefer it this way. I don't like to ask for a loan with all those nosy clerks hustling about, if you know what I mean." The stranger smiled, but there was something in the smile that alerted Oppenheimer. This was no ordinary man.

The bank president put his pen down and leaned back in his chair to look the stranger over more carefully. What he saw impressed him. Clean-shaven, rawboned, the man had a shock of dark brown hair, thick eyebrows, a solid chin, and keen brown eyes that sparkled with amusement. His shoulders were broad and square, his waist almost as supple and thin as a girl's.

With a reluctant sigh, Oppenheimer said, "All right, young man. How much do you want to borrow?"

"Four thousand dollars."

Oppenheimer was astonished. "Four thousand! Why, that's quite a sum."

"It surely is, and that's a fact," the stranger calmly agreed.

"Well now, suppose you tell me what collateral you are offering in exchange for this loan."

"Collateral?" the stranger asked.

"Of course," Oppenheimer replied. "No bank would lend such an amount without collateral. What lands do you own? How much livestock do you possess? It is obvious from your appearance that you are a cattleman."

"I punch cows, all right. But I don't have any land. And my horse is all the livestock I own," the stranger said.

"Then I must tell you frankly, sir, that with all due respect, there is no way in the world that this bank would loan you such an amount. I am astonished you did not know this before you walked in here."

"Oh, I reckon I knew it, all right." The stranger continued to smile at Oppenheimer.

"Then why on earth . . . !"

The stranger's eyes twinkled. "I just wanted to make sure, is all."

"Well, you have just made sure," Oppenheimer responded curtly, making no effort to hide his annoyance. "And now, sir, if you'll excuse me, it is getting late, and I have these books and ledgers to go over."

"Then I won't keep you." The stranger took out his Colt and pointed the barrel at Oppenheimer's chest.

Staring into the revolver's huge muzzle with horror, Oppenheimer scrunched back in his seat, his hands gripping the arms of his swivel chair.

"Why, sir!" he cried. "What is the meaning of this?"

"This Colt is my collateral," the stranger said calmly.

"A single firearm?"

"You might say, its potential for violence," the stranger added.

"You must be mad!" Oppenheimer cried.

"Not mad, just a mite anxious for that loan."

"You would be robbing this bank! The hard-earned savings of men and women. I can't allow that!" Oppenheimer insisted.

The tall stranger got casually to his feet and stepped back. "I don't think it matters anymore what you will or will not allow, Mr. Bank President. Now just open up that safe over there and count out four thousand dollars. I'll give you an IOU for the amount and be on my way."

"An IOU! You *are* mad!"

The stranger spoke with deceptive softness, but his voice carried powerfully in the small office. "Do as I say

12

and keep your voice down." The Colt in his hand gestured to the safe.

"I . . . I'm not sure I remember the combination," Oppenheimer protested feebly, getting to his feet.

The stranger smiled.

With an unhappy sigh, Oppenheimer crossed to the safe, went down on one knee, and began twirling the combination. In a moment, there was a barely audible click as the tumblers fell into place. The president turned to look up at the robber, hoping against hope that this odd stranger was not really serious after all.

The stranger waved his six-gun impatiently.

Swinging open the heavy door, Oppenheimer reached in and pulled out a drawer. Getting to his feet, he lugged it over to his desk and dumped out the sacks of gold and silver coins and the neatly packaged treasury bills. As the treasure spilled out over the desktop, the stranger holstered his weapon, poked through the bills, and began counting out the tens and twenties.

Oppenheimer knew the drawer contained at least twenty thousand dollars in bills and another seven hundred or so in gold and silver coins. Yet after having counted out only four thousand dollars in bills—the same amount he had requested as a loan—the stranger stepped back, apparently satisfied, and stuffed the money into his saddlebag.

Draping the bag over his shoulder, the stranger took the banker's pen, tore off a portion of a page from the open ledger on Oppenheimer's desk, and swiftly scratched out his IOU. Finished, he stepped back and handed it to Oppenheimer.

The banker snatched it angrily and glanced down at it.

To Whom It May Concern:
    I owe the Miner's and Cattleman's Savings and Loan of Gunnison, Colorado, the sum of four thousand dollars.

There was no signature. Instead, Oppenheimer saw a barely legible scrawl that resembled a brand—a Circle D, it looked like. He glared at the robber.

"And you expect me to accept this? You must be mad!"

"It might take a while, but I'll pay it back. All of it," the stranger promised.

"I find that difficult to believe."

The stranger shrugged. He obviously was not at all surprised or offended at the banker's unwillingness to believe him. Taking out his Colt, he moved closer to Oppenheimer, who stepped back in sudden alarm.

"Do you want to be knocked out or bound and gagged?" the stranger asked calmly.

"For God's sake, put down that gun! I promise you—I will make no outcry!" Oppenheimer cringed.

"Sit down."

The banker regained his composure. "All right," he said grimly. "Have it your way. Bind and gag me. And may you be damned to hell for this day's mischief!"

The bank robber produced rawhide strips from his saddlebag. He bound the banker's wrists securely behind his back, then wrapped the rawhide tightly about his ankles. This accomplished, he stuffed a bandanna into the banker's mouth before pulling him from the chair and dropping him not so gently to the floor. Oppenheimer felt his eyes bugging as he tried to catch his breath with the gag in his mouth. He had barely managed to do so before the stranger firmly shoved him deep into the well under his desk.

Stepping back from the desk, Clint Dennison glanced about the bank president's office. The door to the safe still hung open. The top of the banker's desk remained littered with the sacks of gold and silver coins and the bills Clint had not taken. The only visible signs that the banker was still in his office were the tips of his shoes poking out from under the desk. Clint moved the swivel chair closer to the desk, effectively hiding the man's feet from view.

Striding over to the safe, he swung the door shut. He straightened up, listening carefully to the sounds coming from outside the bank. On the main street of Gunnison, the Saturday afternoon traffic clopped and rattled past the bank at a nearly constant volume. There was no sound of activity coming from the alley in back of the bank, and in that instant Clint realized he still had the chance to empty out his saddlebag and leave the bank the way he had come in, an honest man.

For a moment he was tempted to do just that. But only for a moment.

His father's letter, folded neatly, still rested in his inside vest pocket. Its bitter, scrawled message burned into his brain. Four thousand dollars was all the old man needed, and no more. Yet, without it, the ranch he had built up during a long, brutally hard lifetime would be taken from him. Foreclosed. With this money, however, he could once again face proudly, on his own land, the years remaining to him. He would never need to know how his son had procured the money. And he never would.

Turning swiftly, Clint strode from the office, let himself out the rear door of the bank, and mounted the horse he had left tied up a few buildings away. He took the horse at a slow walk through the alley and out onto the street. Only when he was well past the express office on his way out of town did he lift his mount to a lope. But the moment he was out of sight of Gunnison, he urged his horse to a swift, hard gallop.

Chapter Two

Not long after Clint Dennison rode out of Gunnison, Bruce MacDougal climbed up into the box of the stage-coach and watched as his shotgun rider clambered up beside him. Billy was carrying the Greener shotgun, and MacDougal could see how well it was oiled.

"You just keep that weapon at the ready, Billy," MacDougal growled, fitting the reins into his big hands.

The four passengers had already climbed in, and Billy had stored their gear securely in the rear boot, leaving the rack on the stage roof clear, as MacDougal wanted. One look at the two new passengers made the driver appreciate Slim's uneasiness. The girl looked as tough as a horseshoe, and her companion was too big and too soft to make a living honestly. The other two passengers had arrived in Gunnison on the train the day before. One of them, MacDougal had heard, was an actor from Denver. The other passenger, a tall, attractive woman whom he judged was in her late twenties, had the pinched face and bearing of an Eastern schoolmarm.

With a nod to Billy to hang on, MacDougal unfurled his whip and took his foot off the brake. "Gee up!" he cried at his six horses, sending the whip crackling over their broad backs. "Get a move on, my beauties!"

The powerful horses responded immediately, eagerly even. Their muscles knotted as they gathered their feet beneath them and leaned into their harnesses. A few went off stride as they scrambled to get a foothold on the hard ground, but another crack from MacDougal's whip forced the horses to tighten their step and dig in. At once the stage picked up momentum, and in a few moments the horses were lengthening their stride as the stage lurched forward and rattled down the street on its way out of town.

Replacing his whip, MacDougal looked back and waved to Slim, who was standing on the express office porch. Then he turned his attention to the road ahead of them. The stage was riding a bit lower and rocking a little less than usual. It was just as he and Slim had expected, but MacDougal doubted his four passengers would notice.

Inside the stagecoach all Helen Bromfield noticed was how ineffective the leather curtains were. They were rolled up to let in what little breeze there might be, and as a result choking clouds of dust were billowing from the stage's wheels and in through the side window. She pulled away and rested her head against the rear of her seat. Unfortunately, this gave her a clear, unobstructed view of the two passengers who had gotten on in Gunnison—a young woman and an obscenely fat man—who were sitting opposite her.

The woman was dressed completely in men's attire and had been smoking a small, thin cigar since she entered the stagecoach. Her long red curls fell brazenly to her shoulders, like any cheap woman of the night. But even more astonishing to Helen was the revolver the woman wore in a holster around her tiny waist.

She was staring impudently back at Helen, obviously quite aware of Helen's disapproval and not in the least concerned by it. Once Helen had glanced swiftly through a few of the shocking, disreputable periodicals that related the squalid tales of women who had gone West and contrived to abandon all semblance of decent womanhood in the process. She had heard of Calamity Jane, and the pert, small-boned woman sitting across from her was undoubtedly one more example of such depraved womanhood.

Sitting beside the woman was a startling contrast—a man whose girth flowed like soft dough over his gunbelt. He was wearing a filthy red cotton shirt, which was unable to cover his entire paunch. During his wheezing struggle to haul himself into the stagecoach, the shirttail had come out from under his belt, revealing a patch of his white, hairy belly to Helen's horrified gaze. The exposed portion of his anatomy had grown larger as their journey continued, but the man was completely unconscious of it. Like the girl beside him, he was staring rudely at Helen, his small, piggish features almost lost in the swelling suet of his face. He reminded Helen of a gigantic toad.

Shuddering inwardly, she looked away from them both, staring out the window at the tilting, rolling landscape, trying to screen out the stinging dust and the mind-numbing rattle and roar of the stage.

In a kind of dull despair, she asked herself for the hundredth time what kind of people lived in this wild, Western outland. Would the children she was coming to teach be wearing guns, as well? And what kind of protection could she possibly expect in such a coarse, uncivilized society? The trip from Boston had been interminable, but during most of it she had experienced a welcome sense of adventure and excitement, a true joy in leaving Boston behind for the sake of the young, eager children of these brave frontiersmen and women she had read so much about. She had been looking forward eagerly to Cimarron and her duties in the classroom.

However, the farther west she traveled, the more her vague misgivings had given way to a sickening apprehension. The men and women she had observed the last few days had looked so woefully poor—so incredibly drab! While the men were gaunt and sullen, with a hint of desperation in their eyes, it was the appearance of the women that affected Helen the most. They wore no bright colors at all. Their long dresses were unadorned, their hair caught up carelessly under their grim bonnets, a look of dull weariness stamped on their faces—and on the faces of their children, as well. In addition, the towns through which she passed were mean and small, consisting for the most part of unpainted, ramshackle houses, queer false-fronted buildings, and broad, dusty squares and streets. Each dirty, miserable town seemed to have been dropped by an indifferent God into the midst of an awesome, hellish emptiness.

And always—always—there was the enormous distance Helen had yet to travel. For days as she crossed the immense, oceanic prairies, the mountains had hung in the sky above the horizon, seemingly just a few miles ahead of her. Yet, for the longest time, they had remained remote, tantalizingly distant. It was as if the world were turning under her faster than she could travel. In her nightmares she dreamed she was destined to travel forever, doomed like some accursed Flying Dutchman to ply forever the wastelands of this immense continent.

Abruptly, Helen closed her eyes and took a deep

breath. It was not good for her to brood like this, she realized. She told herself she must get some sleep. But the heat was unbearable, the dust maddening, and all she could do was pretend to be sleeping as the rumbling coach lurched up still another interminable grade.

John Ferris was sitting next to Helen. She had not spoken a word to him since taking her seat, and he wondered how long this silent barrier would last. He was well aware of her feelings about actors, and anyone else she thought existed on the fringe of respectability. She was a woman with whom he had no wish to become intimate. But the two of them were sitting together inside a miserably cramped stagecoach in the company of two uncouth ruffians. If nothing else, Helen Bromfield and he should at least attempt to be civil to each other.

Glancing at her, he saw that she was attempting to get some sleep. Considering the heat and the rattle of the stage, he did not see how she could be successful, but he leaned his head back and closed his eyes. Anything was better than staring at the fat man and his girlfriend. Ferris did not know what rock they had crawled out from under, but he would be pleased when they were no longer his traveling companions.

Stirring restlessly, he realized he could use a drink. No—it was more urgent than that. He badly needed a drink. He should not have made that silly vow and stayed away from the hotel bar before the stage's departure. It was his craving for alcohol as much as the heat that caused the beads of perspiration to stand out on his forehead.

Pulling his handkerchief from his breast pocket, Ferris patted his forehead and tried to think of other things. Denver had been a disappointment, but he had heard good things about Cimarron and Montrose, and Grand Junction beyond. His agent had insisted the common folk of those towns would appreciate his one-man show, unlike the gaudy, pretentious citizens of Denver.

The problem was that deep within, Ferris really did not care. Not any longer. More and more, he had been finding it almost impossible to get up in the morning. And so overwrought were his fevered imaginings, so teeming with sick fancies, that at night he could sleep only when he was either completely exhausted or drunk, or preferably both.

Moistening his dry lips, he stirred restlessly and sat forward. More than ever he craved that drink. But he was grimly determined not to give the frigid Bostonian sitting beside him the satisfaction of seeing him reach for his flask.

Ferris took a deep breath and looked out the window at the sun-blasted landscape. Everywhere he looked, the land was as dry as a bone. The brilliant sunshine slanting off the rocks and barren hills caused him to squint. He looked away, leaned back once more, and closed his eyes. As he did so, Annabelle's pale face appeared before him, her luminous eyes peering into his soul.

He almost groaned aloud. Resolutely, he sat up and forced himself to think of something else. Anything else. He simply had to forget Annabelle. He could not survive if he did not. At the same time, however, it seemed senseless— even obscene—for him to survive without her. She had been his life, and he had been hers. What was he doing— lurching across this hellish landscape while her pale, life- less form sank into everlasting corruption?

But at least, he reminded himself, she was rid of that awful contagion—her lovely form no longer consumed by that senseless white plague. What Ferris could never forget

22

was how hauntingly beautiful Annabelle had been at the last. Her pale alabaster brow had shone like a halo. Not death, but life, seemed to glow in her flushed, hectic cheeks, while her ruby red lips clung to his with such a passionate eagerness that when the storm of their lovemaking passed, he could only gaze down at her loveliness in wonder. Never would he be able to forget her clear, brilliant, comprehending eyes. At such times, while she was being consumed by that terrible fire, it was as if she knew all things, past and present.

Abruptly, Ferris began to cough. He snatched out his handkerchief and bowed his head as the terrible spasms racked him. When at last the fit of coughing passed, he pulled away his handkerchief and wiped his lips. Looking absently at the handkerchief before putting it back into his pocket, he noticed a tiny speck of blood. Startled, he looked closer. Yes, there could be no doubt of it!

The white plague—consumption—had found him also!

He took a deep breath and leaned back once more in his seat, glancing quickly about him at the three other passengers. They must have heard his hacking cough. In these close confines, they could not possibly have missed it. But they were deliberately looking away from him.

He was not surprised. What was so momentous to him was of no concern to anyone else in the coach—and certainly not to the world at large. The sublime indifference of mankind was all he had a right to expect, and in that instant John Ferris glimpsed the enormous gulf that yawned between his soul and that of every other person. But it did not matter to him. Not at all. For in the speck of blood in his handkerchief he had seen his deliverance. Perhaps even sooner than he could have hoped for, he would be rejoining Annabelle.

With a thin, bitter smile on his pale, sharp-featured face, he leaned back in his seat, content for the first time in months.

On the other side of the coach Lorna May could only smile pityingly as she watched the two other passengers—the woman pretending to be asleep, the Fancy Dan fidgeting and coughing loudly. They were such hopeless tenderfoots. But that was all to the good, she realized.

From the moment she sat down, she could tell that the coach's floor was higher than it should have been. And that meant Carl was right. It had not been a cracked axle that had kept the stagecoach in the carriage shop all that time. Beneath their feet, just below the double floor that had been installed the night before, was the gold shipment on its way to Cimarron from the Denver mint, just like Carl had told them.

Beside her, Sam Dodge edged his huge rump closer and reached out slyly to take her hand. Lorna May coolly slipped her six-gun from its holster and, cocking it, pointed the muzzle at Dodge's crotch. She did not smile.

Dodge pulled away swiftly, cold sweat standing out suddenly on his pasty face.

Clint Dennison was traveling on foot.

An hour before, his horse had shied away from a rattler, thrown Clint, and gone galloping off into a boulder-infested gully. When Clint caught up to it, the gelding had jammed its right foot between two boulders. The horse might have been all right if it had remained still and waited for Clint to free it. But in its panic, the horse had shattered the bone just above the fetlock and was thrashing in agony when Clint finally caught up to it. Clint had removed his saddle and saddlebag and ended the animal's suffering.

The unpleasant deed was still troubling him as he reached the stage road to Cimarron, his saddle and gear on his shoulder. Clint had once heard an oldtimer say there were only two things a cowboy feared—being afoot and a decent woman. He did not know about the decent woman, but being afoot was sure as hell no pleasure.

As he hobbled along on his high-heeled riding boots, he recalled the wild look in the gelding's eyes a moment before Clint had sent that round into the horse's brain. He wondered if the horse had known that he intended only a kindness in blowing out its brains? He knew only a fool attributed to dumb brutes the feelings and attributes of a human being. The gelding had been in agony and Clint had neatly and simply ended the horse's pain and terror.

Clint hoped that what he had done in Gunnison would turn out to be just as neat and just as simple.

Reaching the crest of a steep grade, he was about to sit down and rest a moment when he heard the rattle of the stage behind him—and above that sound, the sharp crack of a whip. Dropping his saddle, he scrambled up onto a boulder and looked down the steep grade. Yes! The Cimarron stage was climbing the hill toward him, the six-horse team laboring mightily. Clint smiled. His luck was holding.

As soon as the stage gained the crest, the driver pulled his horses to a halt and rested his foot on the brake. He looked down at Clint with a friendly smile, but Clint felt a little nervous as the shotgun rider sitting beside the driver kept his double-barreled shotgun trained steadily on him.

Removing the stub of a cigar from his mouth, the heavy stage driver nodded curtly. "You just out for a stroll, mister?" he asked. "Or are you looking for a ride?"

Clint smiled up at the man. "I lost my horse a while back. A rattler spooked him. I'd appreciate a lift to the way station. I can pay for it."

"Get in then and welcome," the driver said.

Clint thanked him with a nod as the driver said something to the man beside him and took the shotgun from him. The guard climbed down and helped Clint store his gear and saddle in the rear boot. As Clint opened the door to step into the coach, he glanced up to thank the driver again and saw him leaning over, the shotgun still in his hands, both barrels trained on Clint.

The stage started up again so quickly that Clint was thrown roughly into the seat between the window and a prim, straight-backed young lady.

"Would you prefer to sit by the window, ma'am?" he asked the woman.

She was obviously a little surprised that he should ask, but promptly nodded. "Why yes, thank you."

They exchanged places, and Clint glanced around at the other passengers. He was about to introduce himself when he thought better of it. It was no time to be broadcasting who he was. Besides, the other three passengers did not appear to be all that eager to know. He leaned back, content that he was no longer walking. Though he was not safe yet, night would be falling soon. A posse would not be able to pick up his trail until morning.

In a wagon far ahead of the stagecoach, young Ephraim Foster was getting tired. His small arms were drooping, and the two horses were beginning to notice how lightly the reins were being held. Their pace faltered, and they began tossing their heads nervously. Noticing this, Annie glanced over at her son.

"Why don't you let me drive the team now?" she asked the youngster.

Ephraim tried to mask the relief that flooded his face. "Just let me go a little ways farther, Ma," he said. "Until we get to the top of this hill."

"All right."

Marylou had fallen asleep, her head in her mother's lap, and Annie was reluctant to wake her. They crested the hill, and Ephraim pulled the wagon over to the side of the road, reining in the horses. Awakening Marylou gently, Annie lifted the girl off her lap, then moved over and took the reins from Ephraim. The boy jumped down and ran around the wagon, climbing up beside his sleepy sister.

The horses stamped impatiently and turned their heads. They were obviously wondering at this sudden stop.

"Look, Ma," said Ephraim, pointing. "There's Lone Bear!"

Annie glanced up and saw the Indian astride his pony on the flat top of a boulder overlooking the stage road, two or three hundred yards distant. The Indian stood out clearly against the bright sky. The powerful, blocky figure and the single feather in the headband were obviously Lone Bear's. When the Indian realized they had seen him, he waved. Annie and Ephraim waved back energetically. Marylou stirred to life and waved also. Ephraim put his arm around her, and immediately she snuggled against her brother and closed her eyes.

As Annie started the horses again, Lone Bear pulled back off the boulder and disappeared. A quarter of a mile farther on, the Indian rode out from behind a clump of scrub pine and headed toward the wagon. When he reached her, Annie reined in the horses, greeting him with a smile.

Lone Bear was a Cimarron, or Southern Ute. His

chief had been the great Ignacio. Though he was not a member of the northern Ute bands, which a couple of years earlier had participated in the battle of Red Canyon, Lone Bear and his people had been forced to move to a reservation in the Animas Valley south of Durango. However, Lone Bear and a few members of his band had not gone with the rest of the Ute. They had remained in the area—hidden, invisible, ghosts on horseback, haunting the peaks and valleys that surrounded Annie's ranch.

But Annie would have been the last person to tell anyone in Gunnison that Lone Bear and a few of his tribesmen were still in the vicinity. For the past two winters it had been the Indians who had watched over Annie and her children like hawks, twice sending hostile Apaches fleeing when their hunting parties came too close to her ranch.

"What are you doing here, Lone Bear?" Annie asked pleasantly.

"I wait for you," he replied, pulling the Bible she had given him the week before from a leather pouch slung over his pony's neck.

"I have read much in this Bible," he told her. "I find some things in this book very strange. What this book say makes my thoughts go on long, weary chase, yet still I find nothing and must return."

"Is there anything in particular that bothers you, Lone Bear?"

He smiled quickly, his teeth brilliant in his dark, handsome face. "Yes. I will find place. You will help me."

Lone Bear's powerful fingers flipped the pages swiftly. Coming at last to the passage he was searching for, he read aloud rapidly, his voice rumbling powerfully in his massive chest.

". . . And God spoke unto Noah, saying, Go forth from the ark, thou, and thy wife, and thy sons, and thy sons' wives with thee.

"Bring forth with thee every living thing that is with thee, of all flesh, both of fowl, and of cattle, and of every creeping thing that creepeth upon the earth; that they may breed abundantly in the earth, and be fruitful, and multiply upon the earth. . . ."

He halted suddenly and looked up from the page, a frown on his face. "I did not find this to be the speech of my white friends. It sounds strange to my ears. What does 'thee' mean?"

"It means 'you'," Annie explained.

"Then why does not this writer use that word?" Lone Bear asked.

"It was the style of those days to say 'you' in that fashion."

The Indian nodded, but the frown remained. "All that water God send down! For forty days and forty nights. Why did it not drown the insects who live under the rocks? Did Noah search out two of them, also? And the worms that live in the ground, the scorpions that hide in the dark places? Did he find two of each? I think maybe there are too many to find and save. And it does not say in here how Noah would do such a thing."

Annie smiled and sighed, wondering if it had been a good idea to give such an intelligent Indian the Bible to puzzle over.

Two years before, when Lone Bear first entered the

Fosters' cabin, he had caught sight of her late husband's modest library. Like a child in front of a Christmas tree, his dark eyes had lit up, and he had promptly asked Annie if he might borrow a book. Astonished, she asked if he could read, and he had explained that when he was a young brave, his tribe had found a starving, nearly frozen missionary in a snow-clogged pass. The old man lived only a few months, but before he died the following spring, he taught Lone Bear to read.

Of course she had allowed the Indian to borrow a book. It did not take long for her to discover that Lone Bear's appetite for the printed word was all but insatiable. With disheartening speed he devoured every history, biography, and work of fiction in her late husband's library, then began reading Annie's almanacs and mail-order catalogues.

"I think it would be better if you do not try to understand all of the Bible at once, Lone Bear," Annie suggested. "Remember what I said before. Think of it as the story of the white people. My husband was a non-believer, and for this reason he would not allow this book in our home. But, as I said, many white people have found comfort and truth within its pages."

"And have you found comfort also in these many thin pages?" Lone Bear asked quickly.

"Yes, Lone Bear. I have."

"Good. I will go back and read more and return this holy book to you. Then we will talk of it."

"This book you do not have to return, Lone Bear," Annie said. "It is yours to keep. It is a gift."

His dark eyes glowing with pleasure, the Ute nodded solemnly. "Thank you, Annie Foster," he said, his hands clasping the book lovingly. "It is a fine gift. But still it makes my thoughts grow tired. I will need you to help me, I think.''

Then he dropped the Bible back into the leather pouch, swung his pony around, and rode out ahead of the team. Pulling up at their head, he turned and looked back at Annie. He was offering to escort her and the children the rest of the way back to their ranch.

Gratefully, Annie untied the reins from the brake handle and started the horses again.

Chapter Three

Merlin Oppenheimer managed at last to spit the gag out of his mouth and began to shout for help. But the heavy Saturday afternoon traffic outside the bank drowned out his thin, quavering voice.

After a few minutes he gave up calling for help and concentrated instead on kicking his swivel chair away from the desk. Once that was accomplished, he wriggled out from under the desk and began struggling to pull his wrists free of the rawhide looped tightly around them. As the sun's rays crept farther and farther across the office floor, he struggled desperately. Twice he paused in his frantic efforts and called out again. But each time his high, yelping cries aroused no one, and he was forced to continue his painful task alone.

At last he managed to yank free one blood-soaked wrist. It was only the steady flow of warm, slick blood that had made the feat possible. Both wrists were torn from the deep lacerations caused by the unyielding rawhide. After restoring the circulation to his hands, Oppenheimer untied his ankles and stood up carefully. It took a surprisingly long time for the pins-and-needles sensation in his feet to subside. As soon as he was able to, he hurried from his office.

Halfway to the front door of the bank, he stopped—an audacious plan forming in his mind. It was the sweet, effortless simplicity of it that appealed to him. Oppenheimer returned to his office. Closing the door carefully behind him, he ignored the sacks of gold and silver coins still heaped on top of the desk and began counting out the bills the bank robber had left. When he finished, the bank president shook his head in wonderment. There was no doubt about it. The fool had taken only four thousand dollars, leaving close to sixteen thousand dollars behind!

Oppenheimer stepped back and looked down at the neat piles of bills on his desk. Then he turned and walked over to the window to gather his thoughts. What he saw from the window was not a sight to gladden the heart of a poet—and it did not gladden Oppenheimer's heart either. Huddled close to the back of the bank were two unpainted privies. Beyond them, on the other side of the alley, Oppenheimer glimpsed a sorry, sagging rear porch. A torn pair of red flannels was drying on a clothesline strung from one of its posts. Not a single living soul was visible. It was a symbol to him of the dreary wilderness, of the long, lonely years he had spent in the raw community.

It was close to dusk, yet no one had come looking for Merlin Oppenheimer. Though he had failed to return to the widow Palmer's boardinghouse after leaving for the bank early that morning, no alarm had been given. He could have had a stroke and been lying on the floor of his office, dying, and no one would have cared enough to seek him out. Yet, Oppenheimer was perversely proud that not a single person in Gunnison cared enough about him to wonder what might have caused his long absence. His solitary existence gave him an anonymity, an invisibility that he prized. Others might shake their heads in pity, but the bank president only smiled. He counted his wealth, not his friends.

Turning away from the window, he returned to the desk, opened his valise, and quickly stuffed the bills into the leather pockets lining its insides. Then he crumpled the bank robber's IOU and threw it in, as well. Closing the valise, he tightened both straps and carried it over to the wooden clothes closet against the wall, where he lifted the valise onto the upper shelf, pushing it all the way back.

Returning to the window, he noted the position of the sun. It was still almost an hour before sundown. A tight smile on his face, his eyes gleaming like two gold pieces, Oppenheimer decided he would give that fool of a bank robber a little more time to make good his escape. The president of the bank left the window, sat down in his chair, and leaned back to wait.

Sheriff Rex Barney and Sarah Palmer rode into town a little after dusk. When they saw the crowd in front of the bank, they turned their horses and rode closer. As soon as the town constable and Deputy Tim Thornton saw Rex and the widow approaching, they left the low porch in front of the bank and pushed through the crowd toward them.

"What's all this?" Rex asked his deputy.

"The bank's been robbed, Rex!" Tim shouted excitedly.

"When? Just now?" the sheriff asked.

"No, earlier. While Merlin was alone in the bank."

"How much did they get?" Rex asked.

"There was only one man," broke in the town constable. "At least that's what Merlin claims."

Rex saw Oppenheimer standing beside the entrance to the bank. Dismounting swiftly, the sheriff pushed past the two men and mounted the bank's front porch. Oppenheimer's seamed features were indistinct in the twilight, his flinty eyes peering mournfully at Rex.

"What the hell happened here, Merlin?" the sheriff asked.

"I was in my office this afternoon checking the books. You know I always do that on Saturdays."

Rex shrugged. "No, Merlin, I didn't know that. But go on. What happened?"

"A lone gunman broke in and braced me. Took all the folding money I had in the safe, then tied me up and stuffed me under the desk." Oppenheimer thrust out his two wrists. "I just got free a few minutes ago."

Glancing at the man's wrists, Rex winced. The outlaw must have bound the banker's wrists pretty damn tight with rawhide. Where Oppenheimer's skin was not broken through completely, it was raw. "You better get them wrists looked at, Merlin."

"No need for that," the banker said shortly, flexing his fingers. "I'll wash them off when I get back to the boardinghouse."

"How much did the sonofabitch get?" Rex asked again.

The bank president took a deep breath. It obviously hurt him to tell the extent of the bank's loss. "All the folding money I had in the safe, Sheriff. Close to twenty thousand."

Rex was stunned. "My God, Merlin. What's the bank got left?"

36

"Some government securities, mining shares, and sacks of gold and silver coins. We're low, Sheriff. Mighty low. I hope you can bring that outlaw in," Oppenheimer added fervently.

"This happened in your office, you say?"

Oppenheimer nodded. "Come inside, Sheriff. I'll show you."

Rex followed Oppenheimer inside, and the banker lit a desk lamp. Rex inspected the open safe. The lock had not been forced. Small leather pouches containing gold and silver coins were still scattered over the top of Oppenheimer's desk where they had been dumped. On the floor were the bloody strips of rawhide that had bound the banker. Peering under the desk, Rex saw where the dust had been disturbed by the man's struggling body. A few seconds later he saw a tiny drop of blood on the floor left by Oppenheimer's bleeding wrists as the banker struggled to free himself.

Straightening, Rex asked for a description of the bank robber.

"Tall, clean shaven. His hair is brown. He had thick dark eyebrows and a solid chin. Nice-looking man, now that I think of it," he admitted reluctantly.

"What's he wearing?"

"A black, flat-crowned Stetson, Levi's, checked shirt, and a buttonless leather vest," the bank president replied carefully.

"Was he alone?"

Oppenheimer nodded with some assurance. "I'd say so. He talked and acted like a loner."

"That won't make it any easier. What's he packing?" Rex asked.

"A Colt .45," the banker said.

"Strapped down?"

"Nope."

Rex nodded. "Now just when did all this happen?"

"Early this afternoon," Oppenheimer said.

"That means you've been trussed up all this time."

The banker nodded bleakly. "I called for help, Sheriff," he explained with some bitterness, "but no one heard me. I expected that someone—perhaps the widow Palmer—would notice my absence. But no one did. I had to free myself, and that took time."

Rex nodded unhappily. "Sarah and I took a ride out to that horse ranch I'm buying. We just got back."

"Yes, I saw you two ride in." Oppenheimer shrugged resignedly. "Just do what you can, Sheriff. Get that man. He's got our money. And yours, too, I might add."

"I'll get him. You say he rode out about midafternoon?" the sheriff asked again.

"Yes. Not long after, I think I heard the stage pull out."

Rex frowned thoughtfully. "That'll help some, Merlin."

"You going after him tonight?" the banker asked eagerly.

"Wouldn't do much good now. It's almost dark. I'll leave first thing in the morning. Right now I'll ask around. Someone must have seen this fellow in town. That was a good description you gave me, Merlin. It should help some."

"I hope so, Sheriff."

The two men left the bank together. The crowd had begun to disperse, and Sarah Palmer had already left. With a curt nod to the sheriff, Oppenheimer stepped wearily off the porch and walked through the crowd, heading toward Sarah's boardinghouse.

Rex watched him go for a moment, then hurried from the porch to confer with his deputy and the town constable. He intended to visit the livery stable, too. It would help if he could get a description of the horse this lone bank robber was riding.

An hour or so later, on the front porch of Sarah's boardinghouse, Rex Barney leaned back against a porch post and told her what he had found out so far.

"Merlin was right," he said. "That outlaw left Gunnison not long before the stagecoach. Jeff Newman saw him ride out of the alley behind the bank. When he left town, he was heading northwest, toward Cimarron. Soddy Flint saw him, too. Their description matched Merlin's perfectly."

"What was he riding?" the widow asked.

"A big dun gelding. I checked with the livery stables. Johnny Trump didn't remember seeing any horse like it, so it don't look like the fellow stayed overlong in Gunnison. Jeff and Soddy both said they thought this outlaw's dun stepped a mite high, though."

"You mean it's skittish?" Sarah asked.

"Sounds like it. If so, he might give his rider some trouble. I hope so. We need something to slow this outlaw down," the sheriff complained.

"It doesn't sound like you have much hope of catching him."

"I am going to need a lot of luck, Sarah." The sheriff sighed.

Sarah Palmer was sitting in her favorite chair, a wicker rocker. She looked up at Rex and smiled. Where Rex Barney was concerned, she did not believe in luck. He was a man who did not need luck. Not for a moment. And Rex Barney would not come back empty-handed.

She guessed Rex was close to fifty, though he had never told her his age and she had had the good sense never to ask. He had a walrus mustache and a thick white shock of hair that reminded her of snow on a mountaintop. Secretly, she wished Rex would someday trim the mustache slightly, but so far it had proven no impediment when they embraced, and his blue eyes still had the keenness of a knife blade. Broad shouldered, he still moved with the sure, easy grace of a healthy animal.

"You'll get him," she said encouragingly. "I know you will."

"I wish I was as sure as you are." Rex kicked at the post.

"When are you pulling out?"

"At dawn," he said rather unenthusiastically.

Sarah looked beyond Rex and straightened in her seat. "Here comes Tim."

Rex turned and waited silently as the young man mounted the porch steps. Tim greeted the widow with a polite nod, then turned to Rex.

"I want to go with you tomorrow, Rex. Can I?" he asked eagerly.

"The town needs you here, Tim," Rex pointed out.

"The constable can take care of things. I want to go with you," the deputy begged.

"Why is this so important, Tim? It's going to be a hard ride. We'll eat plenty of dust and scald our asses on hot leather—and maybe still end up empty. We have damn little to go on."

Tim grinned. "I sure don't believe that, Rex. But I don't care how hard a ride it is. I want to see how you track this here outlaw. Besides, you're quittin' soon, ain't you? Gonna buy that ranch and settle down. At least, that's what I hear. So maybe I need to see how a real lawman works.''

Rex glanced at Sarah. There was a slight twinkle in her hazel eyes. Rex shrugged and looked back at his deputy. ''All right then, but make damn sure you don't slow me down. Be ready to move out before dawn. Now, git!''

Rex and Sarah watched Tim hurry back down the street. He was a tall, thin, sandy-haired wisp of a young man, all eagerness and good-natured blunder. At times, he reminded Rex of an untrainable hound, pushing his snout into badger holes and scorpion nests. And he read too damn many of the dime novels put out by that Ned Buntline writer. But whenever Rex recalled his own early days crossing the continent and grubbing for gold dust in California, he sighed and admitted that he had been just as raw as Tim and just as eager. If it had not been for a few old-timers with savvy, he would never have survived to be twenty.

Sarah got out of her rocker and moved closer to Rex. In a voice soft with concern, she said, ''Take care of that long-legged galoot, Rex.''

He put his arm around Sarah's waist. It was no longer slim, but it was solid and warm. ''Yes, I will,'' he told her. ''He's my replacement, don't forget.''

She rested her head against his shoulder. ''I won't forget. That ranch is lovely, Rex. And you know how sick I am of this boardinghouse.''

He chuckled. ''I figured you were. But that horse ranch will mean work, Sarah. Hard work. For both of us.''

41

"Mmm . . ." she murmured. " 'For both of us.' That sounds so nice."

He squeezed her affectionately. Rex knew that unless he caught the bank robber, there would be precious few funds left in the bank to support any such purchase. The crook who rode out of Gunnison that afternoon had taken not only the bank's money, but the town's money as well, including Sarah Palmer's and his own.

Despite the fact that MacDougal had driven his team hard, their late start from Gunnison meant the stagecoach did not reach the stage station until late that night. As soon as it pulled to a stop, the weary passengers stumbled out, stretched their stiff legs, then headed through the darkness toward the low log building.

After visiting the filthy privy behind the building, Helen entered the stage station's single large room. She was struck by its barren, primitive look. Like everything else in this depressing land, she thought, nothing appeared to be finished. The furnishings had been fashioned from roughcut timber and pine logs. A huge fireplace, constructed of rough fieldstone, filled the end wall, and above it, rough-hewn shelves contained the cooking utensils. A huge black pot hung over the fireplace. The only luxury was a hand pump. At least the stationmaster's wife did not have to lug in water from the outside well.

The passengers were sitting at pine tables placed along the whitewashed wall. The stationmaster's wife, a thin, sallow creature, was serving the passengers with what meager refreshment she was able to provide at the late hour. She had plenty of coffee, evidently, and its aroma did much to smother the other, less-wholesome smells that filled the dim room.

Helen saw that she could sit with the gun-toting woman and her fat companion or with the actor. For a moment she was uncertain what to do—but only for a moment. When the actor glanced at her, a slight smile lit his face, and it was all she needed. Gratefully, she joined him at his table.

The stationmaster's wife hurried over with a bowl of venison stew, sourdough biscuits, and coffee. Helen found the stew quite satisfying, delicious even. As she pulled her steaming cup of coffee toward her, she glanced up at John Ferris. He had said nothing while she ate, content simply to lean back and watch.

"I guess I shouldn't complain," she said to him, "but this coffee is going to keep me awake."

"I doubt if anything will keep us awake tonight. We're all pretty exhausted."

"I hope so. Sleeping sitting up is no pleasure. But I do need to sleep."

He nodded with a smile. "Ah, yes. Of course you do. So do we all. 'Sleep that knits up the ravel'd sleave of care.' Sweet, blessed sleep." He paused and leaned back to his chair, his eyes growing somber. " 'To sleep,' " he said softly. " 'Perchance to dream: ay, there's the rub; for in that sleep of death what dreams may come. . . .' "

She glanced sharply at him. "I am afraid that is not quite the kind of sleep I had in mind, Mr. Ferris."

His eyes glowed. "Ah, then you are familiar with the Bard."

"Of course. That was Hamlet contemplating suicide, I believe."

He nodded. "Forgive me. I did not know you were so well educated."

"Really, Mr. Ferris. You mean it was not obvious to

you—as it has been to almost everyone else on my journey—that I am a schoolteacher?''

Ferris smiled ruefully. ''I guess I should not have tried to fool you. Yes, of course, I knew. Schoolteachers are one of Boston's most important exports to the West.''

''Yes, Mr. Ferris. I am another one who is hoping to bring to this wild and uncivil land a goodly measure of learning, the enobling refinements of civilization,'' Helen said rather defensively.

Ferris nodded somberly. ''Both sorely needed, I must admit.''

Helen glanced past her companion at the two other passengers. The fat man had been staring at her impudently since the moment she entered the room. To feel the man's eyes moving over her gave Helen a chill, slimy feeling. Shuddering slightly, she looked away.

The mild shudder that passed through her did not go unnoticed by the actor. ''You do not seem to like those other two passengers,'' he remarked.

''Is it that obvious?'' Helen asked, a bit surprised.

''Yes. I am afraid it is.''

''I can't help it. I find them both loathsome. I don't think either one has taken a bath in weeks.'' She wrinkled her nose.

''It's worse than that, I'm afraid. They're dangerous,'' Ferris said.

''Yes. Two cutthroats armed to the teeth.'' Helen sighed wearily. ''I will be so glad to get to Cimarron. This has been such a long—such an interminable—journey.''

John Ferris nodded sympathetically. ''Boston is a long way off, indeed. I imagine as you look back to it and recall its fine cultural amenities, it might seem as distant and unattainable as another planet.''

44

Helen was pleased that he was able to express so aptly what she felt. "You are right. I wonder if I will ever walk upon those narrow cobblestoned streets again, or look out over the harbor . . . and its forest of masts. . . ." She shook her head wearily. "I must have been mad to have embarked on this trip."

Ferris reached out gently and took her hand. She knew she should pull it away immediately, but she did not. His light, friendly touch warmed and comforted her.

"Why then did you make this trip?" he asked gently. "Is there not someone waiting for you in Cimarron? Your fiancé perhaps?"

She smiled faintly, bitterly. "I am afraid not, Mr. Ferris."

"But there must be someone waiting for you," he insisted.

"Oh, yes. The members of the school board will be expecting me, of course. But I have never met any of them. My correspondence has been solely with the head of the school board, a Mr. Ebenezer Wilton."

Ferris studied her closely. She was a handsome woman. As they talked, some of the fatigue that had given her such a wan, fretful appearance had disappeared, and her face had taken on an animation that was pleasant. He liked her eyes the most. They were intelligent and alert. It struck him that she was either very brave to come this far alone or very unhappy—or perhaps both. She was probably fleeing from a personal tragedy, he realized. A man, perhaps. Some cad who had not treated her as such a woman deserved.

"Tell me," he said with a sudden smile, "since you are so well acquainted with Shakespeare, can you place this quotation? It is one of my favorites."

45

She brightened. "Ah, a word game. Yes, by all means. Try me. But I warn you, I am very well read."

" 'Life's but a walking shadow . . .' "

" '. . . a poor player,' " she cut in eagerly, " 'that struts and frets his hour upon the stage, and then is heard no more; it is a tale told by an idiot, full of sound and fury, signifying nothing!' "

He put up his hand to stop her. "Whoa!"

They both laughed.

"Now it's my turn," she said.

Since Romeo and Juliet were her favorite Shakespearean characters, Helen began with the balcony scene. Before she had finished uttering the words, " 'What light through yonder window . . .' " John Ferris broke in and finished the line.

Helen encouraged him to finish the entire speech. She was impressed and delighted with his facility, and in a moment she had forgotten her mean surroundings and the fat man's eyes watching her from the other table.

As Helen and John relaxed in each other's company, Clint Dennison was outside in the stable, busy saddling up the horse he had purchased from the stationmaster. It was a powerful blue gelding that Clint realized at once was a much more solid animal than the skittish dun he had had to leave to the buzzards.

Tightening the cinch one more time, he stepped into the saddle and, ducking his head, rode the horse out of the barn. Yes, he liked the feel of the big animal under him. It would take him far, and it would take him fast. Clint was about to ride out of the yard when the orange glow shining through the stage station's grimy windows drew his attention, reminding him just how much he would appreciate a good cup of coffee.

He turned his mount and rode back across the yard. Dismounting, he dropped his reins over the hitchrail in front of the stage station and entered. The driver and the shotgun messenger had entered before him, so that all the tables were occupied. He walked over to the table occupied by the woman and the actor and asked if he might join them.

He had interrupted them in the midst of some kind of word game, he noticed. But they did not seem at all put out by his request as they looked up quickly, smiles on their faces.

"Of course," the actor said. "By all means, join us."

As Clint sat down, the actor said to him, "Allow me to introduce Helen Bromfield, Mr. . . . ?"

"Just call me Clint," he replied with a smile, nodding pleasantly at Helen Bromfield.

"And I am John Ferris, an actor on tour. A one-man tour, I might add."

"You must find that pretty lonely," Clint suggested.

The actor shrugged. "Of course, but some of these small mining towns and railheads have contained my most attentive audiences."

The stationmaster's wife hurried over to Clint with a bowl of venison stew and a steaming cup of coffee and placed them before him. He thanked the woman with a smile. Dipping his spoon into the savory stew, he sipped it and found it delicious. Before long he was pushing an empty bowl away from him.

Much refreshed, he drank his coffee and looked around. The thin-faced young woman and the fat man were watching his table carefully, he noticed. He did not like the cold look either of them had in their eyes. In fact, he had not liked anything about them from the moment he climbed into the stage.

"Will you be riding on with us to Cimarron?" Ferris asked.

"No. Afraid not," Clint said, glancing back at the actor. "I just made a deal with the stationmaster for one of his horses. He drove a hard bargain, but I was in no position to dicker, and it was a fair price, after all. It is a fine, handsome animal."

"What happened?" Helen asked. "Why were you on foot out there in that terrible country?"

"My horse bolted on me. Broke a leg," Clint answered.

"Oh, how terrible."

Clint nodded. "I was lucky to catch this stage, I can tell you."

His coffee finished, Clint got to his feet and clapped his hat on. Smiling down at them, he said, "You should reach Cimarron sometime tomorrow. Have a pleasant journey, if you can manage it on the stage," he added with a wry grin.

Touching the brim of his hat to Helen, Clint turned and left the station. The stationmaster had just about finished changing the horses. All six animals struck Clint as unusually large and powerful for such a nondescript stagecoach, but he gave it little thought as he wheeled his mount.

As the lights from the station vanished behind him, he found his thoughts going back to the Bromfield woman and the actor—and more particularly, to those two hard cases traveling with them. The fat man and his girlfriend had reminded Clint of coiled snakes getting ready to spring. It was a chilling thought.

Nevertheless, he could not afford to worry about them, he reminded himself bluntly. It was himself he had to worry about. With the day's action, he had become a fugitive from the law. He was an outlaw, pure and simple, and must ride hard to outdistance any posse headed his way. Clapping spurs to his mount, he lifted the horse to a ground-devouring lope that took him swiftly over the moon-lit landscape.

Chapter Four

It was midmorning of the next day when Sheriff Rex Barney and Tim Thornton first saw the buzzards.

Reining in his mount, Rex pulled his hat brim down lower to shade his eyes and peered at the tiny specks of black shifting like giant cinders against the cloudless blue sky. As he watched, the vultures wheeled steadily lower. Their keen, red-rimmed eyes had found a carcass to feed on.

Ordinarily, Rex would not have paid buzzards much attention. The vulture was the prime scavenger that kept the rugged country clean of carrion, and Rex found nothing unusual in the sight of them coasting in the warm updrafts high above the valleys and foothills of this rough land.

What alerted him this time, however, was their large number. He counted seven . . . eight. No, ten. They were dropping to earth beyond a squat mesa at least a mile south of the two riders. To satisfy that many buzzards would take a sizable carcass, a bear, perhaps—or a horse.

Or a man.

Rex Barney knew they would have to turn south to check what the vultures were feeding on, though in doing so they might lose valuable time. Starting out from Gunnison at the crack of dawn that morning, he and Tim had followed the stage road until it cut south. At that point, Rex had discovered a set of tracks that left the road and continued northwest on a direct line through the mountains—fresh tracks made only the day before, since hardly a trace of sand had blown into the depressions left by the hoofprints. Of course Rex could not be sure, but his instincts told him they had found the trail of the outlaw they were after.

He had become even more certain when he saw how deftly the rider had hidden his tracks even while moving at a brisk pace. He had kept mostly to rocky ground, and for long distances stayed on cap rock even though this caused him to drift slightly to the south. Coming to a swift mountain stream, the lone rider had followed its course to the northwest, keeping to the gravelly center of the swift water. Only through luck and Apache-like patience was Rex able to spot the few sandy places close to the shore where the swift water had not entirely washed away the outlaw's hoofprints.

For the past hour, however, they had been following no sign as Rex had kept a steady northeast course through the mountains. And now these buzzards pointed to another possibility.

The buzzards were still dropping. Dinner was on the table. A feast, from the looks of it.

"Rex . . . ?"

The sheriff glanced at Tim. The deputy looked unhappy and discouraged. Rex cut a fresh plug of tobacco with his pocket knife and flipped it into his mouth.

"Yeah, what is it?" he asked.

"You think them buzzards might be feeding on the outlaw?"

"Now, wouldn't that be nice," the sheriff replied. "And laying right beside him, untouched, would be the saddlebags bulging with all that money." Rex shook his head in exasperation. "Hell, Tim! Ain't it a mite soon to be praying for miracles?"

Tim shifted uncomfortably in his saddle and looked away from the scorn in Rex's eyes. "I guess maybe it is, at that."

In a gentler voice Rex suggested, "But maybe it wouldn't do any harm for us to go have a look. Just so we don't set our hopes too high."

Tim nodded and followed Rex, who had swung his horse south.

Before long the two lawmen discovered it was not a man but a horse the vultures were feeding on, their bloody, hooked beaks ripping and tearing at the huge carcass. The younger, less-aggressive buzzards were awaiting their turn on the rocks above, hunched like old women, their eyes fastened greedily on the raw, exposed ribs and flanks of the dead animal. Occasionally, one of the waiting vultures would spread his wings and launch himself from the rocks. A momentary flurry would follow as the newcomer fought for a place and managed to nudge his head through the ring of feasting birds.

Dismounting, the two men picked their way through the narrow gully toward the carcass. The footing was unsteady, the boulders sharp. Rex realized a horse plunging through the narrow gorge would not keep his footing for long. At last the two men were close enough to see the bullet hole in the horse's head. A moment later, using his

53

hat to dislodge a couple of persistent buzzards from the carcass, Rex caught a glimpse of the horse's shattered bone.

From what Rex already sensed about the outlaw they were tailing, he did not believe the man had ridden his horse full-tilt into the treacherous, boulder-strewn gorge. The horse must have bolted. Considering what Jeff Newman and Soddy Flint had told Rex about the mount the outlaw was riding, that made considerable sense.

The lawman took another couple of steps closer and continued to wave his hat at the buzzards. A few more spread their wings and lifted sluggishly off the carcass. Most of the birds, however, paid him little heed as they continued to rip into the dead animal's muscles and sinews. The more aggressive birds had their snouts deep into the intestinal cavity and were gorging themselves on its foul contents. Swarms of flies rippled over the carcass, darkening the bloody flanks. Rex had seen enough. There was no doubt in his mind. The dead horse matched the dun gelding the bank robber was supposed to be riding.

As the sheriff walked to his horse, a few buzzards returned to the carcass to resume their meal. It was a sad sight for Rex Barney, as it would be for any man who loved horses. It was a miserable end for what had been a noble—if skittish—animal.

Tim had a sick look on his face as he hunkered down beside his horse. He plucked a grass stem and proceeded to chew on it, his bleak eyes averted from the buzzards at their meal.

Rex sent a long black dagger of tobacco juice at the ground. "I'd say it was the outlaw's horse, all right."

Tim nodded. "That means the sonofabitch is afoot."

"For now, yes," the sheriff agreed.

"Then we got him!" Tim exclaimed excitedly.

"We sure as hell have an edge."

Tim stood up. "Hot damn!" he said eagerly.

"Easy, Tim. Easy. We ain't got our man yet. We got tracks to look for, man tracks this time."

"So let's go find them."

It did not take long. Circling the area cautiously, they found the outlaw's footsteps almost immediately. His high-heeled riding boots left an indentation difficult to miss. It was Tim who found the first set of footprints. He was grinning as he pointed to them.

Kneeling beside the tracks, Rex nodded. "He's carrying his saddle and the rest of his gear, I'm thinking—judging from the holes his heels are making."

"We'll get him for sure now," said Tim, as he went for his horse.

"Maybe." The sheriff looked up from the ground and peered at the rough trail ahead of them. It was treacherous ground, enough to make a walking man footsore and mean. It also afforded many fine places for an ambush.

"Just keep your eyes up and your Colt loose in its holster," Rex told Tim as he got to his feet and went to his own horse. "If that fellow's up ahead of us afoot, he's liable to be a mite unhappy at this change in his fortunes."

Tim patted his six-gun. "Just give me a chance at him," he proclaimed eagerly as he swung into his saddle. "That's all I ask."

Rex sighed. He did not think it would be profitable to remind his young deputy that was precisely what the outlaw would be thinking the moment he caught sight of two horsemen on his trail.

The sheriff swung aboard his mount, and without a word nudged his horse past Tim's. He was beginning to regret the weakness that had let him take the deputy along. If Rex had to have a companion on the trail, he would have preferred one who was not so up and down, so rollicking sure of victory one minute, so absolutely certain of doom and despair the next—and someone who thought more and spoke less. A damn sight less, as a matter of fact.

About an hour later they were following the outlaw's tracks down a steep trail that led to the stage road. When Rex pulled up on the road a moment later, he pursed his lips thoughtfully.

It was all there in the dirt in front of him, as easy to read as a newspaper: the footprints of the waiting outlaw, the ridged indentations left by the braking wheels as the stage pulled up, and then the unmistakable patterns left by the horses' hooves as they stood restlessly, waiting. Just as clear were the deep indentations their hooves left as they dug in again when the stage pulled out—undoubtedly with the outlaw inside. Just to make sure, Rex rode ahead of the spot where the stage had stopped, his eyes on the ground.

There no longer were any footprints.

Rex pulled his horse around and rode back to his unhappy deputy. Tim was learning fast, and he, too, had been reading the tracks in the road.

"Looks like the sonofabitch flagged down the stage, huh, Rex?"

"That's what it looks like," the sheriff agreed.

"Damn! That'll put him way ahead of us. We'll never catch him now!" Tim sounded as though this new development was a personal insult. "Do you think he'll stay on the stage?"

"Not this one. He'll ride as far as the next way station and buy himself a fresh horse."

56

"Damn it all, Rex. There goes our chance to get him soon," Tim exploded.

"I admit it doesn't look so good. And since he got on this stagecoach last night, he's been riding a fresh mount since before midnight. I figure he's been riding hard ever since."

Tim shook his head in disgust and swore loudly.

Rex looked sharply at his deputy. "Tell you what, Tim. Why don't you quit now and ride back to Gunnison?"

The question startled the young deputy. "Hell, no! Why would I want to do a thing like that?"

"Seems to me you'd feel a whole lot better. You sure are suffering a lot on this ride. And now the outlaw's just slipped plumb out of our grasp."

"That don't matter none. We can still catch him," Tim insisted.

"You sure of that?"

"Stop deviling me, Rex. You know I want to stay on this outlaw's trail with you. I don't care how long it takes."

"Well, then, I suggest you stop puffing and groaning and realize this here ain't no Sunday school picnic. We're tracking an outlaw, not a pussycat. No one said it was going to be easy, and it was you, remember, who insisted on coming along."

"I'm sorry, Rex," Tim said, his face flaming in embarrassment. "I guess I just got my hopes up—despite what you told me."

"I noticed," Rex said dryly.

"But I'll be all right now," Tim promised quickly, afraid the sheriff might really send him back to Gunnison.

"You sure of that? I don't want you to start moaning

the next time we don't get our way. Or whooping and hollering like a kid if we do."

"I'm sure," Tim insisted.

"All right then. We'll head for that way station and see what we can find out. If this outlaw did buy a horse there, we'll know for sure what he's riding, and maybe what direction he took."

Tim nodded eagerly. "And we might get a better description of him, too," he added.

Rex nodded wearily as he turned his horse. That was a little better. Tim was doing some thinking, finally.

As Rex urged his horse ahead of Tim's, he hoped his little sermon would settle his young deputy down a bit. He knew Tim was like any young man, but that did not make it any less difficult to put up with his wild mood swings. In a moment, Rex had lifted his horse to a steady gallop.

The searing morning sun was pouring down on Carl Sutter. Heavy beads of perspiration were rolling down his long, narrow face, and every once in a while he had to mop his cheeks and forehead with his bandanna. The back of his shirt was dark with sweat.

But Sutter was not worrying about the heat. He had more important matters on his mind, such as the newly minted gold hidden on board the Cimarron stage, and what he would do with it once it was in his possession. Lorna May and he had decided they would buy a ranch in California with their share. Sam Dodge had said something about going back east and opening a saloon in New York. Sutter did not care what Dodge did, so long as he disappeared. Sutter was sick of Dodge, and he knew Lorna May was, too.

Crouched high in the rocks above the stage road,

Sutter had a clear, unobstructed view of the road below him. It lifted up a steep grade with the crest coming under his hiding place. By the time the coach reached the top of the long hill, the vehicle would be barely moving, no matter how hard or how often MacDougal used his whip. Sutter had chosen the spot carefully. This portion of the stage route traversed a boulder-strewn badlands, a baked landscape of towering rock shapes and mesas—the ideal location for what Sutter had in mind.

Sutter's Winchester rifle was resting on the boulder in front of him. He could smell the oil baking in the hot sun. He had taken his Colt from its holster and placed it alongside the rifle in case he needed it in a hurry. As Sutter waited, he could hear his horse cropping steadily on a small, shaded patch of grass behind him.

Then he heard another sound—the distant jingle of harness and the rumble of the coach's wheels on the hard-packed roadway. Hastily, he snatched up his Colt and dropped it into his holster. Damn! It was almost hot enough to detonate the cartridges in their chambers. Even the walnut grips stung his hand. Then he reached for his Winchester and flipped off the safety. The searing metal of the breech singed his hand.

From around a massive boulder far below, the stagecoach swung into view.

Sutter grinned as he saw MacDougal get to his feet in the box and send his whip snaking out over the backs of the six horses. The stage was going at a fairly good clip as it started up the grade, but it did not take long for the horses to begin laboring on the steep slope. Sutter could hear MacDougal shouting at his team, doing his best to urge the horses on. They were big, powerful brutes, and they kept a surprisingly good pace for most of the climb.

But just as Sutter had expected, they were struggling, and the coach had slowed almost to a crawl by the time it neared the crest.

Sutter tucked the stock of his Winchester into his shoulder and waited patiently for the stage to get closer. Billy was cradling the Greener shotgun in his lap. Sutter grinned. A fat lot of good that was going to do the mealy-mouthed sonofabitch. Sutter curled his finger carefully around the trigger and rested his cheek almost lovingly on the warm stock. He felt no qualms at all at what he was about to do.

Ever since he was a kid, Carl Sutter had wanted only one thing—to become a stage driver. He knew that in order to become one, he first would have to serve an apprenticeship as a shotgun rider. But when the job as shotgun rider opened up a few months back, it was MacDougal who had seen to it that Billy got the job instead.

Not only did MacDougal keep Sutter from getting the job, he went out of his way to make it clear to the owner of the stage line that he did not think Sutter could ever be trusted for such a job, after which he had proceeded to proclaim loudly in every saloon along his stage route that Carl Sutter would never make a stagecoach driver, that he did not have the hands and sure as hell did not have the guts.

Sutter rested his Winchester's sights on Billy's head, then lowered them to his chest. The time had come to see who had the guts. Billy's chest loomed as big as a barn door in the gun's sights. Sutter squeezed the trigger. The rifle barked, the recoil biting into his bony shoulder. As the crack echoed in the surrounding rocks, Billy flung up both hands and toppled backward off the stage.

The frantic driver sawed back on his reins and pulled the stage to a sudden, rattling halt. Sutter yanked his bandanna up to cover the lower portion of his face and stepped out from behind the boulder. MacDougal, his six-gun in his hand, had turned to look back at Billy's body, sprawled face up in the road.

"Drop that six-gun, MacDougal!" Sutter cried.

Whirling, his face white with shock and fury, MacDougal glared at Sutter. "You murderin' sonofabitch! You killed Billy!"

"Yes," the outlaw drawled, levering a fresh cartridge into the Winchester's firing chamber. "I guess I did, at that. And there's another bullet here for you if you want it. Drop your gun, I said."

MacDougal let his weapon fall to the ground.

Clint had ridden through the night, staying just ahead of the stage, which had left the way station not long after he did. Close to dawn, however, he had found a stream and watered his horse, at the same time allowing himself an hour's rest. During his short nap the stage had passed him. Since that single break, he had been riding steadily, heading for Cimarron and his father's ranch fifty miles farther west.

For the last few miles, he had left the stage road and kept to the ridges above it. Not too far ahead of him, he knew, was the stagecoach, and occasionally he would glimpse it on the road below. He would start to gain on it, only to lose sight of it again as the driver came to a downgrade and let out his horses.

Clint made no effort to overtake the stagecoach, however. It would mean too punishing a pace for his new mount, and in the blistering heat he wanted to make damn sure he kept a healthy horse under him.

He was riding through the still, oppressive morning heat and was looking for a shady spot for himself and water for his mount. As he rode, he paid little attention to the now familiar sounds of the stagecoach rattling along the road and the dim shouts of the driver and the sharp crackling of his whip. Easing his mount up a steep, shale-littered trail, Clint realized the narrow trail he was following doubled back and took him away from the road toward a pine-studded ridge to the north.

As he crested the ridge a few minutes later, he heard the sharp report of a rifle. The shot came from behind him. He pulled up instantly and turned in his saddle as the detonation rolled like thunder off the surrounding rocks. Clint listened intently as the ominous echoes faded, but he could no longer hear the familiar rattle of the stage—and instantly he knew why.

Wheeling his horse, he rode back off the ridge, heading for the stage road.

The rifle shot alerted John Ferris as well. Launching himself from his seat, he poked his head out the side window of the coach just in time to see the shotgun rider tumble past him to the ground. Abruptly, the stage slid to a halt, slamming Ferris forward so violently he almost catapulted through the window. Holding on to the window frame to steady himself, he peered at the road and saw a masked figure step out from behind a boulder above the roadway, a rifle in his hand.

It was a holdup!

From behind him, Ferris heard Helen gasp.

"All right, actor," the fat man's gravely voice said. "Haul your ass back inside this coach."

Ferris pulled his head in and slumped back into his seat. Both the young woman and her companion had drawn their weapons, and Ferris found himself staring into the cavernous muzzle of the fat man's revolver. Suddenly cold sweat stood out on his forehead. From beside him Helen gave a tiny cry of terror. Ferris reached out quickly to comfort her. She seemed almost paralyzed with fear.

"Don't worry, Helen," he told her, taking her hand. "All they want is that strongbox under the driver's seat."

"Shut up and get out, both of you," snapped the woman. The cold menace in her voice was startling to hear from one so young.

As she waggled her gun menacingly, Ferris opened the door and stepped down, then turned to help Helen out. Crowding behind them came the fat man and the woman.

"Get back against the stage and keep your hands in the air," the fat man told them.

"That's really not necessary," said Ferris, stepping protectively between the man and Helen. "I am not armed and neither is this woman."

"Damn you! You just do like I tell you!" cried the fat man, clouting Ferris on the side of the head with the barrel of his big Colt.

The blow rocked Ferris backward, and he almost fell to the ground. Groggily, he turned and backed up against the stage, both hands held in the air. Helen, apparently sobered by what she had just seen, took her place meekly beside him.

The masked outlaw was returning from inspecting the sprawled body of the shotgun rider. As he reached the stage, he lifted his rifle so that it was trained on the driver, who was still in the driver's box, staring down grimly at the three highwaymen.

"Throw that strongbox down, MacDougal," the masked man cried, "then come on down yourself. Just don't do anything sudden."

The driver tossed the box over, then clambered down. The fat man kicked the box upright, then aimed two quick shots at it. The padlock flew apart. The big fellow waddled over, threw back the lid, then dipped his hands into it, hauling out three sacks of coins.

Straightening, he chuckled and looked at the masked man. "Pretty good for a start, I'd say."

"It's just the frosting on the cake," said the woman coldly. "Let's get this stage out of here."

The masked man nodded. "Sure, Lorna May. But first, why don't you see what valuables these two passengers are carrying?"

Lorna May moved like a cat. Snatching Helen's purse from her, she pawed swiftly through it, taking what little jewelry and coins she found. She snapped off a gold pendant hanging around Helen's neck. Stopping in front of the still-dazed Ferris, she reached deftly into his inside coat pocket and withdrew his bulging billfold. Ferris cursed bitterly as she pulled out a few of the bills and held them up for the others to see.

"Drop the loot in the strongbox," the leader told her. Turning to the fat man, he said, "Dodge, throw the strongbox into the coach and get rid of them mail sacks."

As soon as Lorna May had dropped what she had taken from Helen and Ferris into the steel box, Dodge closed it and hefted it into the coach, then reached in for the mail sacks and pulled them onto the ground.

Watching the three outlaws, a chill came over John

Ferris. This ugly business was not as simple as it had appeared at first. He was not witnessing just another stage-coach holdup.

"Stand over there with them other two, MacDougal," said the masked highwayman coldly.

"Damn your hide, Carl Sutter!" the stage driver said angrily. "I know it's you behind that mask. I'd recognize that voice of yours anywhere!"

With a short, triumphant bark of laughter, the high-wayman pulled down his bandanna, revealing a long face and a feral grin that sent a shiver up Ferris's back.

"That's right, MacDougal," admitted Sutter. "It's me, all right. Carl Sutter. And I've come for that gold you got hidden under the floor of this here stagecoach. Real clever you was, making that double floor, but you didn't fool nobody."

"Take the damn gold, for all I care. But let me go see to Billy. He might still be alive," the driver begged.

"No, he ain't. He's dead all right. I just made sure of that."

"Then may your bones rot in hell, Sutter! You are a cold-blooded murderer!" MacDougal shouted.

"Yes, I am," Sutter acknowledged calmly.

He raised his rifle and fired point-blank at the stage driver. The round caught MacDougal in his chest and sent him slamming back against the right front wheel of the stagecoach. Clinging to one of the spokes, MacDougal stared wildly at Sutter. Sutter levered a fresh cartridge into his firing chamber, aimed, and fired again. The second slug caught MacDougal higher in the chest. He sagged sideways, then crumpled to the ground.

Suddenly Helen was in Ferris's arms, sobbing, her

face buried in his shoulder. Ferris himself felt sick to his stomach.

Without comment, Lorna May opened the stagecoach door and climbed in. As Dodge started to get in after her, he said something to the woman that Ferris could not overhear. Glancing back at Helen, Lorna May listened for a moment, then shrugged. Dodge turned from the stage and strode over to Helen, a yellow grin on his porcine face. Slapping Ferris roughly to one side, he took Helen by the arm and pulled her toward the stage with him.

"No!" Helen screamed, struggling furiously. "Let me alone! I won't go with you!"

The fat man slapped Helen on the face, shocking her into silence. Then he pushed her roughly ahead of him toward the stage. But Ferris grabbed Dodge's shoulder, spun him around, and punched him in his enormous gut. It was at best only a futile gesture, as Dodge's oversized gut swallowed up Ferris's fist easily. He might as well have been punching a huge batch of fresh bread dough. However, Ferris continued his attack, raining blows at Dodge's face and head.

But Dodge simply smiled, brushed aside the actor's flailing fists as easily as if he were dealing with a swarm of mosquitoes, and with casual brutality slammed his Colt down on top of his head. It felt to Ferris as if the mountains all around the stage had collapsed onto him. The ground rushed up and struck him in the back, then tipped crazily under him. Through painful, throbbing eyes, he watched as the fat man thumbcocked his Colt, then aimed carefully down at him.

There was no doubt Dodge was going to shoot Ferris. And the actor was so dazed, all he could do was accept his fate. He closed his eyes and waited for the bullet's smashing, obliterating impact.

But when the shot came, it was a distant one.

Opening his eyes, Ferris saw Dodge drop his six-gun and clutch at his right arm as he staggered back. He was staring up at the rocks above the road, from where the rifle shot had come.

"Let him be!" cried Sutter as he clambered swiftly up into the driver's box and untied the reins from the brake handle. "Get inside now, damn you, or I'll leave you here!"

Still clutching his shattered arm, Dodge shoved Helen into the stagecoach ahead of him, then climbed in after her. Even before he had pulled the door shut, the stage was rattling off—with the gold shipment and Helen Bromfield inside.

Chapter Five

Dismounting, Clint Dennison examined the dazed actor. There was a bloody patch on the top of his skull, but he was conscious and seemed healthy enough. He would carry around an extra lump on his head for a while, but that would probably be the worst of it.

John Ferris blinked quizzically up at Clint, then pushed himself to a sitting position and began to rub the top of his head. "It was you who shot Dodge," he said, squinting painfully up at Clint, who nodded. "Where in the hell did you come from?" Ferris got carefully to his feet.

Clint shrugged. "I heard the shot that stopped the stage."

"That shot also killed the shotgun rider," Ferris said. "Now they've got Helen—Miss Bromfield."

"I know," Clint replied, looking in the direction the stage had gone.

"So when do we start after them?" Ferris asked, somewhat impatiently.

"We?"

"Of course!"

Clint decided not to argue with the man. Instead, he left the actor and walked over to inspect the shotgun rider. The young man was still sprawled face up in the middle of the road, his blue eyes staring sightlessly at the bright sky. There was a neat, black hole where the bullet had entered his chest. When he struck the ground, the back of his skull had crunched down on a sharp stone imbedded in the roadway. He must have been killed instantly.

Clint took a step back, reflecting gloomily on the young lad's fate. One minute he was flying backward, the sky twisting above him. The next instant he was plunged into an eternal night. A quick way to go, possibly, but surely the young man deserved more time on this earth. After all, it had been the only chance he would ever get.

Leaving the dead shotgun rider, Clint walked over to the stage driver. With two bullets in him, the driver was long gone, his heavy body sprawled crookedly forward, his face in the dust. A dark patch of blood was still spreading under him.

John Ferris, brushing the dust off his narrow-brimmed hat, joined Clint. "I guess I was pretty lucky," the actor said.

"You were at that."

"What do we do now?" Ferris asked.

"We take care of these corpses," Clint told him. "We'll have to drag them over to the side of the road and cover them up as best we can. Can you help?"

Still somewhat groggy, Ferris nodded. "I can manage."

They had no shovels. After they dragged the bodies to the side of the road, they piled stones on top of them to keep off the coyotes and vultures. By the time they were finished, they had erected a sizable cairn.

"Now do we go after the stagecoach?" the actor asked.

"I'm still thinking about that," Clint replied. "You got any idea who did this?"

"I certainly do," Ferris said.

"I'm listening."

"The leader was recognized by the stage driver. His name's Carl Sutter. Those two passengers, Lorna May and the fat man, Dodge, were in it with him. There's a gold shipment on that stage. It's hidden under the floor," Ferris explained quickly.

During his brief stay in Gunnison, Clint had heard talk of a shipment of gold on its way from the Denver mint. It had come in on the train, some said, its destination the booming copper mines in the mountains behind Cimarron. Because of the staggering inflation rates in the mining camps, the miners had come to mistrust the value of paper currency and insisted on being paid in gold, and this shipment was it. Other townsmen were equally certain there was nothing to the rumor.

But it seems there had been a gold shipment, after all, Clint thought.

"There's no horse for you, Ferris," Clint said. "Sorry. I'll have to ride after the stage alone and see what I can do. Your best bet is to walk back to the stage station and get help."

"I insist on going with you. I must see to Helen's safety."

Clint did not laugh outright, though not doing so was difficult. How in hell did the itinerant actor possibly think he could see to Helen's safety? A fat lot of good he had done her so far.

71

"I told you. I only have one horse," Clint pointed out again.

"But we could ride double!" Ferris suggested.

"In this heat, we wouldn't make any time at all. And it might finish my horse for good," Clint said.

"And so you propose to send me back to that stage station on foot. Is that it?"

Clint looked at the actor. A slim, pale fellow, his dark eyes burned with a curious intensity. Clint was sure the man could hold an audience from the stage, but the sun-blasted badlands was no stage. It was a tough, deadly world he was strutting about in, and this poor shadow of a man in his dusty cape and white spats was woefully out of place in it.

Which meant Clint could not possibly send John Ferris back on foot, after all. The stage station was too far. The silly actor would simply never make it.

"That highwayman who drove the stage," Clint said. "Carl Sutter. I didn't see his horse tied to the stage when he drove off."

The actor chuckled grimly. "No, you didn't. After you shot Dodge, Sutter was in too much of a hurry to think of his horse."

"Then his mount must have been tied up around here somewhere while he robbed the stage. Suppose we find it. Can you ride?" Clint asked.

"Yes, of course I can ride. And I can handle a revolver, as well." Ferris sounded insulted by the question.

This time Clint allowed himself a slight smile. "That so?"

"Yes, it is so," the actor replied patiently. "Now let's go find that horse."

"Hold it," Clint said. "Not so fast. It could be

anywhere among these rocks, and we could spend a lifetime looking for it. Did you happen to see where Carl
Sutter was placed when he fired on the stage?''

''Up there,'' the actor said promptly, pointing to the
rocks directly above them. ''The shot came from those
rocks, and it wasn't long after that I heard Sutter telling
the driver to drop his gun. I was looking into the muzzle of
Sam Dodge's gun at the time, but I heard Sutter clearly
from inside the stage.''

''Then we'll look up there first.''

They climbed into the rocks and found Sutter's horse
with little difficulty. The small, powerful chestnut was still
saddled.

Clint allowed Ferris to lead the horse down the steep
trail to the stage road, watching carefully how the man
handled the chore. He seemed quite at ease with the horse.
When they reached the stage road, the actor turned and
gave the chestnut an appreciative inspection.

''A fine-looking animal,'' he said, adjusting the
stirrups.

Ferris stepped confidently up into the saddle. To Clint's
surprise, the actor sat the chestnut well. Indeed, with his
black cape flowing behind him, he was almost impressive.
If they were riding across a stage, Clint told himself, John
Ferris would do nicely.

Mounting his own horse, Clint rode ahead to pick up
the coach's tracks. Once he found them, he lifted his blue
to a gallop, his caped companion keeping up without
difficulty.

Huddled inside the coach, Helen glared at her two
captors. The paralyzing fear that had assailed her when the
robbery began had given way to fury. Because of the two

barbarians sitting across from her, two brave men were dead and John Ferris had been fearfully beaten. Though he remained alive, it was only through some miraculous intervention. She had no idea who the rifleman was who had shot the fat man, but had it been a lightning bolt from God, she could not have approved more.

The fat man—she had heard him called Dodge by the others—was sitting across from her, clutching his bleeding arm. The bullet appeared to have entered his right arm, just below his shoulder. He was muttering unhappily as he stared balefully at her. Perhaps he blamed her for his current agony. If so, she was pleased. Anything that made him unhappy made her feel better.

"Your name is Lorna May. Is that right?" Helen asked the young woman.

Lorna May shrugged in acknowledgment.

"Then I would thank you to put down that gun, Lorna May. You don't need it. I am not going anywhere, and besides, if I jumped out of this coach, I am sure it would not bother you in the least."

Lorna May looked coolly at Helen for a moment, then uncocked her weapon and holstered it.

"Thank you," Helen said.

The woman smiled thinly. "You're right. I don't care what you do. Go ahead and jump out if you want. It's Sam here who's taken a shine to you, not me."

"Shut up, Lorna May," growled the fat man, scowling at her through his pain. "You and Carl got your diversions. I want mine."

"What you need is a doctor," snapped Helen, facing Dodge. "But I trust you will not find one out here in this godforsaken wilderness, and that encourages me to hope you will soon die of your wound. Nothing would make me happier.''

Sam Dodge leaned over and slapped Helen roughly with his meaty left hand. Her head rocked back. She did not cry out as she sat up again, her eyes stinging.

"Brute!" she snapped, her voice trembling with anger. "That's all you are. A dumb, fat brute."

For a moment Helen thought Dodge was going to strike her again. But he did not. Instead, he leaned back in his seat, still clutching his bleeding arm, and closed his eyes.

"You're lucky he just slapped you," said Lorna May. "If I was Sam, I'd chuck you out of this stagecoach—just to watch you bounce."

"Yes. I imagine you would," Helen said, staring at Lorna May coldly, unflinchingly. At last the young woman turned away from Helen's contemptuous appraisal and looked out the window at the landscape sweeping past.

Helen leaned back and closed her eyes. She was amazed at herself—and at the fury that prompted her to goad the two outlaws with such arrant disregard for her own safety. Her defiance, she realized, was fueled by her anger at what they were and what they had done. And anger at herself as well for getting into such a miserable predicament in the first place—for thinking she could run away from that silly unpleasantness with Paul Washburn.

Recalling the preening fop with the oversized bow tie and receding hairline who had broken their engagement, she cringed inwardly. How could she have allowed a worm like that to fill her with such despair? *My God!* she thought. *I even contemplated suicide!*

She writhed inwardly. Such a silly fool she had been.

Now, out in the great American wilderness, she knew just how much of a fool.

Opening her eyes, Helen glanced out the window at the broken, untamed landscape through which the stage was careening. They had left the road some distance back and were rumbling along a narrow, twisting trail through a land of towering rocks and steep-sided, winding gullies, a crude terrain that seemed to be taking a great deal out of the stage—and the horses as well, judging from the way they were stumbling. She heard Sutter lashing at the six horses furiously. His fury alone, it seemed, was what kept them struggling on through this treacherous land.

Suddenly Sutter pulled up the horses. The coach's wheels began shuddering as they burned against the brake shoes. In a flurry of harness and blowing horses, the stage rattled to a halt.

Sutter appeared in the stagecoach doorway. "All right," he cried. "Out of here! We got work to do!"

Dodge, protesting as he held onto his shattered arm, eased himself from his seat and stumbled out into the blazing sunlight. Lorna May indicated with a sharp nod of her head that Helen should get out ahead of her, and Helen complied. As she stepped down, Sutter moved grudgingly aside. Helen kept going and found some shade beside a huge boulder. She turned to watch Lorna May step down from the coach and join the two men.

Indicating Helen with a motion of his head, Sutter asked Dodge, "Now what the hell are we supposed to do with her?"

Dodge moistened his fat lips. "I'll take care of her," he muttered doggedly.

"I say put her to work," Lorna May replied. "Sam

ain't going to be much help. He's been whimpering like a sick dog ever since he took that bullet.''

"You got any idea who that sonofabitch was who shot Sam?" Sutter asked.

Lorna May shook her head.

"Well, it was bad luck for Sam and worse for us if we let the man catch up to us before we get this gold out of here."

Sutter turned to Dodge. The fat man's face was shrunken and pale. It was obvious he had already lost a considerable amount of blood. He reminded Helen of a hog being slaughtered clumsily.

"You're going to have to help, Sam," Sutter told Dodge. "I don't care how bad you're hurt."

"I'll help, damn it!" Dodge bleated. "I'll help! You can't say I don't pull my weight. But you got to do something about this wound! It hurts something fearful!"

"Later. Once we get this gold out of here," Sutter insisted.

Grudgingly, the wounded man nodded.

The two men, with Lorna May assisting, released the coach's six horses from their traces and led them over to the side of the trail. There, behind a mound of boulders shielded by a tangle of scrub pine, Sutter had already cached saddles and gear. With Dodge giving them less and less help, Lorna May and Sutter saddled three of the horses and placed leather packsaddles on the others. Leading the horses with the packsaddles over to the coach, the three outlaws entered the coach and tried to pry up the stagecoach's floorboards with a blunt shovel blade. The task went depressingly slow, and after a particularly violent wrench by the impatient Sutter, the shovel handle snapped.

In a fury of frustration, Sutter flung the broken handle from the coach, nearly striking Helen. Dodge climbed out and collapsed wearily in the shade of a pine, and Sutter and Lorna May followed him, turning to survey the stage balefully.

"What now?" she asked.

"I've got an idea," Sutter said.

Lorna May just stared at him.

"We'll send the coach down this grade," Sutter said. "It'll break up when it hits that canyon wall at the bottom. Then we'll pick it clean."

Lorna May walked over the crest of the trail and looked down. She studied the canyon wall below for a moment, then shrugged and walked back to join Sutter.

Sutter turned to Helen and ordered her to give them a hand. For a moment, Helen seriously considered refusing— but only for a moment. She realized it would be wise for her to go along, at least for the time being. Sutter called Dodge over as well. Protesting feebly, the wounded man struggled to his feet and joined them behind the coach.

The stagecoach was perched on the crown of the trail. They did not have to push far to get it over the crest. But nudging the stagecoach the few feet necessary turned out to be a difficult task. The gold shipment hidden under its floorboards gave it an added inertia.

Under Sutter's surly goading, the four of them strained until at last the stage eased forward a few feet, and then a few feet more. That was enough. A moment later it was rumbling down the trail under its own gathering momentum.

The four stood back to watch. Groaning like something alive, the coach picked up speed as it headed for the canyon wall and certain destruction. But halfway down the trail, the right front wheel struck a boulder. The wheel swung about violently, and the entire coach veered to the right, struck another boulder, and appeared to leap into the air. When it came down, it was tumbling headlong into a narrow ravine.

The stage was disintegrating as it went. What remained intact finally crunched to a halt in the middle of a pile of boulders at the bottom of the ravine. With a groan, Dodge slumped wearily to the ground. However, Lorna May and Sutter plunged swiftly down the steep slope to the floor of the gully. A moment later Helen could see the two of them poking among the wreckage.

Before long, Sutter and Lorna May clambered back up to the trail. Arousing Dodge with a few judicious kicks to the rump, Sutter went off with the wounded man to get the horses, while Lorna May grabbed Helen by the arm and started to pull her down the slope.

Helen yanked herself free of Lorna's grasp. "I won't go down there!" she said. "Why should I help you outlaws?"

Lorna May swore viciously and hauled out her huge revolver. Cocking it, she said, "You can stay up here if you want, but you won't be breathing if you do."

Grudgingly, Helen followed the woman. She did her best to keep on her feet, but twice she lost her footing and went sprawling headlong down the rough, gravelly slope. By the time she reached the bottom of the ravine, she had lost her hat, and her skirt was torn in several places.

The stagecoach was a sad, broken shambles. Scattered all around it on the ground, like bright dandelions, were gold pieces that had broken free of the stage when it struck. Wasting no time, Lorna May clambered into the coach's interior and began throwing out onto the ground the sacks of gold that were still intact.

"Get in here and help!" she demanded.

Helen crawled into the wrecked stage and began reaching under the splintered floorboards for the gold. As she lifted out the pouches, she was astonished at how heavy pure gold was.

They were still lugging the gold from the stagecoach when Sutter and Dodge arrived with the horses. They had come the long way around, leading the horses up the ravine on foot. At the sight of the pile of leather bags filled with gold and the loose coins strewn on the ground near the coach, Sam Dodge let go of the two horses he was leading and ran the few remaining yards to the gold. Puffing heavily, he slumped to the ground and snatched up a bright coin with his good hand. Biting on it to test it, he pocketed the coin gleefully, then fell upon the other loose coins, grinning at Sutter as he gathered them.

Pulling up alongside Dodge, Sutter looked down at him. "Feel better now, do you, Sam?"

"All this gold sure does make this arm of mine feel better—and that's a fact!" Dodge was almost drooling.

"All right. You pick up them loose coins then. Put them in a couple of the aparejos after you take a bit of the straw out to make some room. We'll split them coins later. Lorna May and this here woman of yours will help me load up the packhorses."

Helen's heart froze when she heard herself referred to as Sam Dodge's woman. She almost protested, but realized how futile that would be. Soon, she was helping Sutter and Lorna May tie the sacks of gold over the straw-filled leather aparejos, which were strapped to the horses to cushion the load. Positioning the load properly was a ticklish task, Sutter told her roughly, since the heavy gold had to be evenly balanced or the packs might shift, and the horses would be unable to proceed.

Sutter and Lorna May worked swiftly, but Helen went as slowly as she could, hoping to delay them somehow. If she could hold them up long enough, perhaps that unknown rifleman who had already wounded Dodge would overtake them and free her. It was a desperate hope, but it was the only one she had. Feigning clumsiness, she kept dropping the gold pouches. Finally, one of them struck a small rock and split open, spilling out its gold coins.

"Damn you!" cried Sutter, striding over to her. "I been watching you! You dropped that gold on purpose! Do that once more, and I'll cut you open for the buzzards and leave you here for them to feed on!"

It was a preposterous threat, Helen thought. But Sutter was clasping the handle of a huge knife as he spoke. She nodded and bent swiftly to pluck the gold coins off the ground, comforted somewhat by the knowledge that until the three outlaws recovered every gold coin scattered about, they would not leave the ravine.

Their greed might yet undo them.

Clint Dennison and John Ferris had wasted no time. Following the coach's tracks, they came at last to the spot where the stage had paused. Dismounting, they studied the ground and realized the stage had been pushed down the trail without its team of horses. With Clint leading the way, they followed its tracks and saw where it struck the rock and careened off the trail. Peering down the steep incline, they glimpsed the shattered stagecoach far below— and the four tiny figures moving about it.

The two men led their horses back off the trail and

tied them up. Ferris had no weapon, so Clint gave the actor his revolver and kept his Winchester rifle for himself. Carefully they worked themselves down the steep slope.

When they got close enough to see the four people clearly, Clint paused to study the situation. Three of the stage's horses were being used as packhorses, and Helen Bromfield was being forced to help load the gold. She was not working with any great enthusiasm, he noted. But the highwayman Clint knew to be Carl Sutter and the young woman, Lorna May, were making up for Helen's lack of speed as they rapidly loaded the bags of gold. The wounded fat man was on his hands and knees, picking up and stuffing in an aparejo the loose coins that had apparently spilled from the stage when it struck the ravine floor.

"Go around behind them, Ferris," Clint told the actor, indicating the far slope with a nod of his head. "Stay in that patch of scrub pine when you cross over. Come out behind those rocks on the other side of the stage. Wave your hat when you're in place. I'll watch for you."

"What will you do then?"

"When I see you're in position, I'll fire on them. I'll aim for Sutter first and try to catch him low. Then I'll see if I can wing the woman. I figure the fat one is already carrying enough lead for now. If my aim is bad and they break back for the stage, that'll give you a clear shot at them," Clint said.

The actor's face paled. "You mean we're just going to open up on them without a warning?"

"What the hell do we want to warn them for?" Clint asked incredulously. "They've already killed two men and would have killed you if I hadn't come by when I did. If we waste any bullets, or call out to them, they'll just grab Helen and use her for a shield. They'll make us drop our weapons, and we won't have any choice but to do it. Do you have any idea what they'll do to us then?''

The actor swallowed unhappily. ''All right. But suppose I sneaked close and rescued Helen? Then they couldn't use her for a hostage.''

''For Christ's sake!'' Clint said in exasperation. ''You'd be a dead man sure if you tried anything like that. You've been reading too many Deadeye Dick novels. This is the real world. Just do as I say.''

Ferris nodded reluctantly.

Clint saw the uncertainty in Ferris's manner, and he did not like it. ''Now listen here, actor, if your heart's not in this, go on back up there and leave this to me.''

''No,'' Ferris said with sudden resolve. ''I want to help.''

''You sure?''

''Dammit, I'm sure. And stop calling me actor,'' Ferris said.

''All right, then. Do you remember what I want you to do?'' Clint asked.

''Yes.''

''Get moving then. Looks to me like they'll be pulling out soon, so hurry it up,'' Clint urged.

Keeping his head low, Ferris hurried off, heading for the other side of the ravine. As soon as he was out of sight, Clint moved closer to the overturned stage, looking for a likely spot to rest his rifle. He found it behind a boulder less than a hundred yards above the floor of the ravine. He levered a fresh round into his rifle's firing chamber carefully, so as not to alert those below him.

As he crouched behind the boulder, he occasionally caught a word. Helen was saying nothing, and the fat man, no longer packing the gold coins, was sitting on the ground, using his bandanna to fashion a sling for his right arm.

Peering at the rocks just beyond the stagecoach, Clint waited. The packhorses appeared to be loaded. Sutter walked over and hauled the fat man to his feet. There were only three saddled horses, Clint noted, which meant that they intended for Helen to ride double. If she rode with the fat man, that would have to be some horse, he thought with a smile.

Clint looked back at the rocks behind the stage. *Where in hell is that actor?* he wondered.

A shot rang out from somewhere among the rocks. At once Sutter grabbed Helen and pulled out his six-gun. Lorna May ducked down behind a boulder, and the fat man crawled closer to the stagecoach, keeping his bulk low. Flinging the woman up in front of him, Sutter spun to face the rocks.

"Who's up there!" he cried.

There was no response.

"I'll kill her!" Sutter cried, holding his six-gun up to Helen's face. "Whoever's up there, back off! I'm warning you. I'll kill the woman!"

"Do what he says, Ferris!" Clint shouted as he got to his feet and stood in plain sight. "Back off! Get the hell out of there!"

His arm still around Helen, Sutter whirled to look up at Clint. "Who the hell are you?" he demanded.

"That's not important," Clint told him. "Don't harm the woman, and we'll both of us ride out. That's a promise. Just don't harm the woman."

"All right then," Sutter cried. "Vamoose! But throw your rifle down, or I'll kill her."

Clint had already turned, however, and was scrambling swiftly back up the steep slope. He had not gone far before Sutter and Lorna May began firing at him. The rounds fell short, but they added a certain urgency to his flight. He reached the trail just as Ferris broke into view farther down.

The two men went after their horses, mounted up, and rode off, heading back the way they had come.

After a half mile of hard riding, Clint pulled up and turned to Ferris.

"You want to tell me what happened?" he demanded angrily.

"I stepped on a rattler and fired without thinking," Ferris said.

Clint looked at the man for a full moment, then decided he was telling the truth. "Did you kill the rattler?"

"I missed. But the gun flash seemed to discourage him."

Clint nodded unhappily. Ferris's answer satisfied him. The same thing had happened to him once, only the gun flash had not helped him any.

"Clint, how come you didn't throw down your rifle like Sutter told you?" Ferris asked. "He had his gun right against Helen's head."

"As long as we were busy hightailing it out of there, Sutter had no reason to worry about me—and no chance to argue the matter."

"But Sutter might have killed Helen," Ferris protested.

"If he did that, we'd have turned on him. And he knew it. This way, he's still got Helen to use as a hostage."

Ferris sighed wearily and nodded. "Now what?"

"We trail them at a safe distance and wait for our chance. But this time, actor, please—don't shoot at any rattlesnakes."

They rode back carefully. Leaving the trail sooner than before, they descended to the ravine and came out near the shattered stagecoach. The four people had already left. From the depth of the hoofprints left by the heavily laden horses, Clint could see the packhorses were struggling under all the gold.

Clint rode along the ravine, following their trail. If Sutter and his party camped for the night, Clint and the actor might be able to sneak close enough to free Helen. But it sure as hell was not going to be easy separating her from the outlaws.

"Suppose they're waiting for us?" Ferris asked, spurring his horse up beside Clint.

"Oh, they'll be waiting for us, all right. They've got to figure we'll be following them."

"Won't that make it dangerous?"

"Sure it will. You got any better idea?"

"No," Ferris admitted.

"Then let's just ride and keep our eyes open."

As Clint rode, he found himself wondering what in the hell he was doing teaming up with a Shakespearean actor to go after three highwaymen and a schoolmarm. Clint was now a genuine, fourteen-carat outlaw himself, and more than likely he was not too far ahead of an irate posse. By rights, he should be making tracks for his father's ranch. That's what he *should* be doing.

But as soon as he considered cutting and running, he asked himself what his father would do in a similar situation—and he knew at once that he had no choice but to stay with the actor and keep after the woman hostage. It did not matter what this course of action might cost him. His father would never walk away from trouble—or a chance to help out a fellow human.

Clint could do no less.

Chapter Six

Annie Foster, with Lone Bear still escorting her, reached her ranch late in the afternoon. As Lone Bear dismounted, she reined in the team and got wearily down from the wagon. Both children had slept well under the stars the night before and were delighted to be free of the wagon's confinement. They scrambled down from the front seat and did their best to help Annie unload the supplies, while Lone Bear unhitched the team and led the horses into the barn without a word.

At last, as the two children raced off to feed and water the chickens, Annie walked out onto the low front porch and collapsed into her rocker. Thunderheads were building in the sky above the badlands. The clouds had been piling up since noon, and in the short time she and the children had been unloading the wagon, the air had grown quite heavy and sultry. She could feel the storm coming and was grateful it had held off until they were home. The narrow canyons of the badlands could be very dangerous in a cloudburst.

After tending to her horses, Lone Bear had set his pony loose in the corral in back of the horsebarn and was walking across the yard toward the house. Annie noticed he was carrying the Bible with him.

Mounting the porch, Lone Bear sat in the wicker chair facing her and leaned back, his dark eyes on her, the Bible resting on his lap.

"It's always such a tiring trip to Gunnison," Annie told him, smiling. "I'm glad it's over. Thank you for meeting us, Lone Bear."

He nodded solemnly and waited impassively. He saw her weariness, and out of consideration for her had decided not to mention the Bible in his hand unless she did so first.

Sighing inwardly, Annie realized she really had no choice in the matter. He had met her and the children primarily to gain an opportunity to discuss with her what he had been reading.

"Lone Bear," she asked, "is there something more in the Bible you want to discuss?"

The Indian nodded, his eyes glowing at once with the excitement that always came on him during their discussions. Swiftly he leafed through the Bible until he found the passage he wanted and began reading aloud to her. Leaning back in her rocker, Annie listened intently. The passage dealt with the destruction of Sodom and Gomorrah. When Lone Bear had finished reading, he looked quickly up at Annie and asked how the Lord could have killed all those people, saving only Lot's family.

Annie immediately felt out of her depth, but she could sense Lone Bear's genuine perplexity and was anxious to allay it. "The inhabitants of those two cities were very wicked," she explained. "They deserved to die. But

Lot was a righteous man, so the Lord made an exception in his case.''

Lone Bear leaned back in his chair, his eyes alight. "Ah!'' he said. "They were wicked, very wicked?''

"Oh, yes,'' Annie said.

"Why? What did they do, these people in the cities?''

Annie felt herself blushing. In truth, she was never very certain herself what crimes the citizens of Sodom and Gomorrah had committed, though she was vaguely aware that it had to do with fornication and other acts of licentiousness, difficult for her to imagine, and none of which she was anxious to discuss with Lone Bear.

"I only know that they were wicked, Lone Bear. They . . . did things that were an abomination in the eyes of God. They displeased him and persisted in their evil ways,'' she finally said.

Lone Bear nodded solemnly. "I have seen such cities with my own eyes, when the white men come together to dig gold and silver from the ground. And when they come to build the rails for the iron horse, they also make such cities. The women who come to these places are as bad as the men. They drink the firewater with the men, and these women will have as many men as can pay them. I have seen it. Yes, your God must not like such places.''

Annie hoped Lone Bear did not notice how she was blushing. Quickly, she nodded. "Yes, Lone Bear. That's what Sodom and Gomorrah were like, I am sure.''

"And that is why the Lord consumed them with his fire?''

"Yes,'' Annie assured him.

"But was Lot's wife not a good woman?'' Lone Bear asked.

"Yes, of course she was.''

91

Lone Bear frowned. "Then why did the Lord turn her into a pillar of salt?"

"Because she looked back at the cities while they were being destroyed," Annie said patiently.

"Is it such a sin then to look back and see the Lord's destruction?" The Indian was obviously struggling to understand such behavior.

Annie tried to explain. "The Lord told Lot that he was not to look back, that no one in his family was to look back. When Lot's wife looked back, she disobeyed the Lord, and so He punished her."

"I think your Lord must be a cruel master," Lone Bear said with great sadness—and compassion—as he closed the book.

Anxious to end this unnerving discussion, Annie said with finality, "Lone Bear, you must understand that the Lord must be like a parent to his children. He must punish them if they disobey."

"I would not turn any of my children to salt if they disobeyed."

"You do not have children," she retorted irritably.

"No," the Indian replied sadly, "I do not."

At once Annie was sorry she had spoken so thoughtlessly.

"You must forgive me, Lone Bear," she told him gently. "I am still tired from the trip. And sometimes I myself do not understand the Bible or the ways of the Lord," she admitted with a slight smile.

He relaxed and sat back in his chair, grateful for her explanation.

Sometimes the powerful Indian's sensitivity amazed Annie. "Lone Bear," she asked suddenly, "why don't you take a woman? I have seen some of the young girls of your tribe. They are very beautiful.''

Lone Bear's face went cold. ''The squaws say Lone Bear's head is full of strange things, and his words are much strange. They say he will never keep food in a squaw's lodge or bring furs to keep her warm in the winter. They say he is not a warrior, because all he can do is read the white men's words. So now the squaws laugh when Lone Bear asks for them to live in his lodge.''

''That is too bad,'' Annie said, genuinely moved by his answer. ''You must be very lonely.''

He shrugged his powerful shoulders. ''Lone Bear is not alone when he reads. He hears the voices speaking to him from the pages. And he is not alone when he comes to this ranch and talks of what he reads with Annie Foster.''

''I'm glad, Lone Bear,'' Annie said as Ephraim and Marylou returned from the chicken coop at a dead run.

''When's supper, Ma?'' Ephraim asked, charging up onto the porch. ''I'm hungry!''

Marylou came after Ephraim and swiftly climbed into her mother's lap.

''Me, too,'' she said, twisting her head to look up at her mother.

Annie laughed and got to her feet. Still holding Marylou's small hand, she started back into the house to cook supper. Then she looked back at the Indian. ''Lone Bear, would you join us for supper?'' she asked.

''What will Annie Foster make for dessert?''

''Apple cobbler,'' she said at once, aware it was his favorite.

''Lone Bear will stay.''

Getting to his feet, he put the Bible down in the chair and looked at the children. ''Lone Bear will take you two for ride on his pony. While your mother make us fine supper, you will not think of your stomachs.''

Long used to these rides, Ephraim and Marylou agreed instantly—and loudly. Lone Bear lifted Marylou onto his shoulders, and with Ephraim at his side, they started for the corral.

Watching them go, Annie suddenly frowned as an alarming thought occurred to her. Were Lone Bear's visits to her ranch solely for the purpose of discussing the books he read? And what about her? Why had she given him that Bible? Why had it become so important to her that he know about it—and through it the religion of her people? Was it because she was beginning to think of Lone Bear as more than just a friendly Indian? As a suitor, perhaps?

The thought was too unnerving for her—frightening, even. She sat back down in her rocker, her heart pounding in confusion. How could she possibly think of herself as Lone Bear's squaw?

At the way station where Clint Dennison and the Cimarron stage had stopped for a meal, Sheriff Rex Barney and Deputy Tim Thornton had obtained not only a good description of the bank robber they were tracking, but of the weapons he was carrying and the horse he was riding. To Tim, however, this was small comfort. They seemed no closer to apprehending the outlaw than they had been the day before.

It was not that Tim did not respect Rex's skills as a tracker. But the sheriff was so frustratingly silent and uncommunicative. He just kept riding, saying nothing, his eyes on the trail. Whatever it was he saw, he kept to himself. How could Tim possibly learn from Rex if the sheriff would tell him nothing and show him nothing?

And Tim did need to learn from Sheriff Barney. Soon, if things went the way he wanted, Tim would be the new sheriff of Gunnison County. Everyone knew Rex wanted to take off his badge, marry the widow Palmer, and settle down on the ranch he was buying in the hills north of town. Then all Tim would need would be Rex's recommendation and the job of sheriff would be his.

That meant Tim would get a raise and would be able to marry Jill Harrison. Until Gunnison had learned of the sheriff's impending resignation, marriage was something he and Jill only dared dream about. But finally it was real and getting more real with each passing day. And Tim wanted to marry Jill more than he wanted anything else. Even riding through the badlands with Rex, the thought of Jill Harrison sent a warmth surging through him that at times left him breathless. Recalling the kiss she had given him when he rode out with the sheriff, Tim could almost feel the warmth of Jill's body as she pressed against him, the taste of her lips on his.

Abruptly, the sheriff stopped.

"What's up, Rex?" Tim asked.

"He's turned back," the sheriff said, pointing to the tracks he had been following. "And in one hell of a hurry. Let's go."

Astonished, Tim pulled his horse around to follow the sheriff. He had been watching the ground, but there had been so many footprints, some going one way, others going another. At times the ground had become a frustrating, confusing tangle of tracks, and Tim had despaired of being able to winnow out the hoof marks left by the bank robber from all the traffic. Yet, all this time, the sheriff had kept them on course.

A few moments later, Tim dismounted on a ledge above the stage road and kept behind the sheriff, who was following fresh footprints past the rim rocks and down the slope for a distance of approximately twenty yards. They could see the stage road below them clearly. The sheriff stopped, bent down, and picked a spent bullet casing off the ground.

He glanced at it, then handed it to Tim. "Winchester .44. Same rifle our bank robber is packing."

Glancing back at the ground, he followed the bootprints back to the rim of the canyon. "He mounted up again here," Rex said. "Let's go. We'll follow him. He's on his way down to the stage road, I'm thinking."

Leading their horses, they followed the bank robber's footprints down a winding, narrow game trail until they came out a hundred yards below the spot from which he had fired his rifle. The two lawmen mounted their horses and turned up the road, the sheriff urging his mount to a lope. For the first time Tim noticed lines of concern etched in the sheriff's face.

When they sighted the stone cairn by the side of the road, they rode toward it. Dismounting swiftly, Rex walked closer to the cairn, frowning. An unpleasant odor hung close about the rocks.

"From the size of this cairn," the sheriff said thoughtfully, "I'd say there are two people under here. But that bank robber only fired one shot."

"Who do you think is buried under there?" Tim asked uneasily. The smell was so bad he was reluctant to join Rex beside the cairn.

"There's only one way to find that out," said the sheriff. "You willing to help me do that?"

"Anything you say, Rex," Tim agreed unhappily.

"Let's make it fast, then."

The two men clawed at the boulders. It did not take long to uncover MacDougal's ghastly face—and then that of the young shotgun rider, Billy. Swiftly, the lawmen piled the stones back on top of the bodies.

Tim thought for a moment he was going to be sick. As he struggled to regain his composure, the sheriff walked slowly out onto the road and began studying the tracks he found there. After a while, he went down on one knee in order to study an impression more closely.

"Here's where one of them lay," the sheriff called out to Tim. "The bloodstain looks reasonably fresh."

Tim walked over, confused. "Dammit, Rex! What happened here?"

"Don't you know?" Rex asked, looking up at Tim in surprise.

"Sure. The stage was held up. But if MacDougal was killed, who took the stage? Where's it gone to?"

The sheriff stood up. "It was driven off, Tim. The highwaymen who shot MacDougal and Billy must have driven off. No trick to understanding that."

"But why?" Tim asked.

"Gold."

"Gold?" The young deputy was genuinely surprised.

"That's right. A shipment fresh from the Denver mint. The express company had some fool notion they could hide the gold under the stagecoach's floorboards. I thought it was a crazy scheme. And it sure as hell didn't fool this bunch, looks like. They've driven off the stage to a place where they can rip it up in private. Then they'll probably use the team for packhorses," the sheriff explained.

"Do you think that bank robber was a part of it?"

"No, I don't," Rex said thoughtfully. "Like you just saw, he shot only once. More than likely, he came on the holdup and fired down at the highwaymen."

"Now why would he do a thing like that?" Tim asked.

"How the hell do I know?" The sheriff followed two pairs of footprints over to the rocks lining the stage road. "I'm just reading sign. And that ain't much help in reading a man's mind."

Tim followed Rex, joining him as he followed the footprints up the slope until they reached a narrow ridge overlooking the stage road. Rex stopped behind a large, flat-topped boulder and bent to pick up another cartridge. He handed it to Tim.

"It's from a Winchester, too," Tim said, examining it quickly. "A .44/.40 caliber."

"Right," said the sheriff. "But we know this fellow we're tailing is carrying a .45 caliber Colt and a Winchester .44. Now who do we know who packs a .44/.40 caliber six-gun and Winchester?"

"Carl Sutter," Tim replied at once.

The sheriff nodded, then studied the ground behind the boulder. "See how this ground has been tramped down? Waiting behind this here boulder for the stage to show, Carl Sutter must've got a mite restless. I figure he fired down on the stage to stop it. That was probably when he killed MacDougal—or Billy. He hated them both, sure enough. And maybe it was that shot which brought the bank robber we been tailing."

"He heard the shot, you mean."

"That's what I mean—and that's why he came so fast," the sheriff explained.

"And then he fired down on the stage, too?"

The sheriff looked at Tim for a long, pained moment, then shook his head. "Ain't you been taking any of this in, boy?"

"Sure, I have. But maybe this bank robber thought it would be a good idea to join Sutter," Tim suggested.

The sheriff shrugged wearily and moved past Tim up the slope onto a small patch behind some boulders. Following the sheriff, Tim saw the droppings at once. The sheriff bent to examine the grass where it had been cropped short.

Straightening, the sheriff said, "Sutter tied his horse here while he waited for the stage."

Tim nodded. That, at least, was obvious.

Rex pointed. "Now look there. Remember the tracks of them two we followed up here? There they go again. This time, they're leading this horse back down through the rocks to the stage road."

"You mean Sutter left his horse here for them?"

"Not for them. He just left it. He didn't need it after he took the stage. He had the stage's six horses, and maybe others waiting for him somewhere in the badlands. A man stealing a shipment of gold gets to feeling mighty prosperous."

Though Tim did not see any of it as clearly as the sheriff did, he nodded and said, "Sure, I can see that."

"Now, who do you think these two were?" Rex asked.

"The two who came up and took this horse?"

The sheriff nodded.

"It must have been two of Sutter's gang," Tim suggested.

"You think so, do you?"

"Who else could it have been? The bank robber we been following has his own mount." The young deputy could see no other alternative.

"Think a minute, Tim," the sheriff urged. "Who did

the stationmaster say was in that coach when it pulled out of the way station?''

''A fellow in a cape, a woman he thought might be a schoolmarm from back east, and two hard cases. One of them was a girl packing a Colt, and the other was a big fat tub of a man.''

''And which of them four passengers do you think might possibly be Sutter's accomplices?'' Rex asked.

''The last two. The girl and the fat man.''

''Yes. And I wish to hell I had been in town when they purchased tickets and rode off in that stage. I've got a wanted poster in my office on that girl from the federal marshal in Durango. Lorna May's her name. And that fat man is Sam Dodge. I'd bet on it. Them two have been causing unhappiness south of us for a couple of months now. It looks like they've come north to join up with Sutter.'' The sheriff shook his head ruefully at the lost opportunity to apprehend the two crooks.

''So what's that got to do with who made the tracks we followed up here?'' Tim asked.

''These tracks were not made by the girl and the fat man. They aren't light enough for the girl or heavy enough for the big fellow. And the heel marks don't match Sutter's.'' Rex smiled and bent to point to one of the heel marks.

''See where a piece of this right heel is broken off on the inside? You can catch it if you look close. That's the man we been trailing, our bank robber. The other footprints I don't recognize, but they're not from a riding boot. This one's wearing fancy dress shoes. See here? Them flat heels leave a nice sharp cut. I'd say they were bought recently—in Denver probably—and I'll bet they belong to that passenger with the cape. He's an actor, or some such, according to what the stationmaster said, and these here shoes are what a feller like him'd be wearing.''

Looking down at the tracks, Tim saw clearly everything the sheriff had pointed out to him. He thought a fellow sure as hell had to be sharp-eyed and as patient as an Indian to see it all in the first place. No one horse's hoofprint or shoe imprint was complete. The same print would be partially made at one point, and then you would have to keep going to find the rest of it later on. Only then could the complete print be pieced together.

As Tim followed the sheriff back down to the road, he shook his head. It sure as hell was not going to be easy to fill Sheriff Rex Barney's shoes. Some folks said Rex was part Apache, and Tim was just about ready to believe it.

Once they reached the road, the sheriff inspected the ground around the cairn again, then showed Tim where the man had mounted the horse he had taken from the rocks. Next he pointed out the spot where the bank robber had mounted, after which the two had ridden out, following the stagecoach. They were the last tracks that had been made.

"Looks to me like our bank robber has ridden out after the stage, and he's taken the actor with him," Rex said, a puzzled frown on his seamed face.

"But why would he do a thing like that?"

"You remember who was in that stage beside the girl, the fat man, and the actor?" the sheriff asked.

"Sure. The schoolmarm."

"You ain't seen any sign of her around here, have you?"

Tim thought for a moment before shaking his head. "Nope."

"She could be dead, sure enough, and buried somewhere up there in the rocks out of sight. But I doubt it. Looks to me like Sutter and them other two brought her along with them when they took the stage. They're maybe fixing to use her as a hostage—or worse. Anyway, that might explain why this feller we're after and that actor are now chasing the stagecoach," the sheriff suggested.

"Hell, Rex. I don't see how you can see all that from reading a few tracks," Tim protested in frustration.

"I know. It don't seem right, does it? And truth is, maybe I got it all wrong. But I can't help it if that's what them tracks show me."

"What else do they show?" the deputy asked.

"That cairn we saw. Know who it was dragged those bodies over there and loaded them stones onto them?" Rex asked.

"No."

"It sure as hell wasn't Sutter and his two friends. It was the actor and our bank robber that did it. Them two made plenty of tracks, and there isn't any chance I could mistake their tracks now," the sheriff insisted.

Tim shook his head. "I still can't figure it."

"What can't you figure?" Rex asked.

"That bank robber we been tailing," Tim said.

"You mean he isn't acting the way he should. Is that it?"

"Yeah." Tim kicked at the stone in the road thoughtfully.

"You got a point, all right," Rex agreed. "Why would an outlaw on the run join up with this actor to save the schoolmarm?"

Tim nodded emphatically. "That's right. It don't make no kind of sense, Rex."

102

"I know it doesn't. But I've been noticing things about this fellow we've been tracking. He just isn't the typical bank robber."

"Maybe he ain't, but he damn well took that money," Tim pointed out.

Rex nodded and mounted up. Without waiting for Tim, the sheriff turned his horse down the road, following the tracks left by the bank robber and the actor.

It was close to sunset, and the two lawmen were deep into the badlands before Rex finally dismounted near the crest of the narrow trail. Tim swung off his horse and joined the sheriff. There was so much activity visible in the dust that it was obvious Sutter had reached the place where he intended to strip the stage of its gold. Tim saw the heavy traffic heading toward a tangle of rocks and oversized boulders on the other side of the trail. Following Rex into the boulders, he looked around, but saw nothing. Then Rex bent and picked up what looked like a fistful of hay. It was fresh and had the spring of curled hair to it.

"Any idea what this is?" the sheriff asked.

"Sure. It's hay."

"A special kind of hay, Tim. Aparejo hay. It's used to pad aparejo packs. Notice how springy it is. That's the way it's got to be, so it won't pack together."

Tim knew what an aparejo was—a leather packsaddle stuffed with hay, on which supplies were loaded. He had never had occasion to use one, but he knew what they looked like. He had seen many a grizzled prospector leading a string of mules with such packsaddles on them.

Rex looked around. "This is where Sutter must have cached his gear and the packsaddles he needed to haul away the gold." Rex scratched the back of his neck.

"Which means the stage should be around here somewhere, stripped clean. Go back out onto that trail there and see if you can find the stage's tracks, Tim. See where it went. I want to poke around here some more."

Tim walked back to the middle of the trail, found the tracks left by the stage, and followed them. He kept going over the crest of the trail. A third of the way down the hillside, he saw where the stage had veered suddenly to the right after striking a boulder. Peering into the ravine below the trail, he caught sight of the wrecked stagecoach far below. Excitedly he called to Rex.

"After a plunge like that, Sutter should've had no trouble at all getting the gold out. The stage is cracked open like an eggshell," Rex said, looking down at the remains of the stagecoach.

"Maybe he sent the coach over on purpose," Tim suggested.

"Maybe." Rex studied the ravine for a moment longer, then straightened up. "Let's get down there before it gets any darker and see what we can find out."

A clap of thunder suddenly rattled the mountainside. The two men looked skyward. Dark, tumbling clouds were rolling swiftly, and with them came a cold gust of wind. Just in time, Tim snugged his hat down securely as large drops of rain splattered all around them. As the heavy raindrops began thudding down onto the brim of Tim's hat, he could think of only one thing: What would they do if the rain kept up for any length of time? If that happened, they would have no more tracks to follow.

Helen Bromfield could not bear the smell of Sam Dodge, nor his manner. Unfortunately, when the darkness had finally forced them to halt for the night and to set up camp, Carl Sutter had insisted that Helen look after the fat man's wound.

Sitting close to the fire with his back propped against a boulder, Dodge was muttering unhappily as Helen slowly cut away the sleeve of his shirt to examine his wound. She was using a rusty pair of shears Lorna May had taken from her saddlebag. As Helen worked, Dodge occasionally stopped his muttering and managed a lewd grin. She tried not to notice.

She pulled the filthy cotton shirt-sleeve off Dodge only to find the equally filthy sleeve of his red longjohns under it. It was encrusted to the wound, and though she cut carefully, it was only with considerable difficulty that she managed to separate the undersleeve from the scabbed-over wound. Sam Dodge was no longer grinning at her.

"Dammit!" he whispered hoarsely. "Go easy, woman!"

Helen ignored him as she flung both filthy sleeves into the fire and looked back at the wound. The campfire's flickering, uncertain light gave her little help, but even so, what she saw was enough to sicken her. The upper fore-arm had been chewed up badly by the bullet, and in the short time since Dodge had been hit, his wound had festered. The smell turned Helen's stomach—along with the stench from Dodge's filthy clothes and unwashed body. The man could not have bathed in a fortnight or longer. It was no wonder his wound had gone septic so quickly.

She pulled back, noting the ridge of pustulant flesh and broken tissue around the wound's edges. At the center of the wound was a black, angry hole. She realized there might still be a bullet in Dodge's arm, but she had no way of knowing for sure. The wound had begun to scab over, and greenish fluids were oozing out from under the scab.

"I'll need to clean out your wound," Helen told Dodge, getting to her feet.

There was a small spring in the rocks just below the camp. She took a pan from the fire, threw away the coffee which had been boiling in it, then filled it with fresh water and brought it back to the fire.

When she returned to Sam Dodge the man had dozed off. Helen thought of what she would need in addition to the hot water. She would need cloth first to swab out the wound and clean it as best she could. Then she would need more strips of cloth to wrap around the wound to keep it clean.

Sutter and Lorna May had wandered off into the rocks above the camp, taking their bedrolls with them. What they were doing at the moment, Helen had more than a good idea. But it did not matter to her if she disturbed them in their play. Their help was needed if she was to clean out Dodge's wound—if she was to save his life, in fact.

As she clambered up into the rocks in search of the couple, she realized how sultry the night had become. She had heard distant peals of thunder while they were making camp and had noticed the dark clouds swirling above them. But the air had become intolerably heavy—electric, even. Perspiration streamed down her face as she climbed farther up into the rocks.

Suddenly she came upon Sutter and Lorna May. They were locked in a lascivious embrace under a blanket. Helen cleared her throat to get their attention. Lorna May said nothing as she leaned back, her small mouth slack, her eyes closed. Swearing softly, Carl Sutter lifted himself from the girl's body and turned to look at Helen.

106

"What the hell do you want, schoolteacher?" he asked crossly.

"I need your help," Helen said firmly.

"Why?"

"I think we should wash out Dodge's wound. It is already septic," she explained.

"Septic?" Sutter demanded. "What in blazes are you talkin' about?"

"I am sure Sam Dodge has blood poisoning. His wound is the source of the infection. If the wound is not cleaned out, he will die."

"Is the bullet still in his arm?" Sutter asked.

"I have no idea."

Sutter laughed. "Go on back to Sam. Wash out his wound if you want, but don't bother us."

"I need some clean cloth." Helen was determined not to be gotten rid of until she had what she needed.

"Take some sheets from Sam's bedroll for bandages," Lorna snapped irritably. "And then leave us alone, damn you."

"That's right," Sutter said, the loathsome suggestiveness of his smile making her cringe. "Just keep Sam company, why don't you? Be nice to him. That's all he needs, I'm thinking."

Helen spun away furiously. They did not care a whit for Sam Dodge, only for their own squalid pleasures.

When she reached the wounded man, she found him still asleep. Or was he unconscious? She placed the back of her hand against his cheek and found he had a raging fever. As she pulled her hand away, Dodge's eyes flew open. He reached out with his left hand and snatched her arm in a grip of steel.

He laughed, his foul breath almost overpowering her

as he pulled her closer. She struggled and tried to beat him off, but his strength was frightening.

"I'm going to take you, schoolteacher," he told her roughly. "Yes, ma'am, that's what I'm goin' to do!"

"You're a sick man!" Helen cried. "I must clean out your wound! Please! Let me go!"

"Hell! It feels better already," the fat man muttered, attempting to roll his enormous bulk over onto her. "Besides, I don't want to die and leave you a virgin. That wouldn't be fair, now would it?"

"You smell!" she cried, frantically twisting her face from side to side as he tried to kiss her. "You are an abomination!"

"My, you do know them big words, don't you," Dodge said, laughing at her struggles.

Glimpsing the scissors lying near the fire, Helen reached out and snatched them up with her right hand, then plunged the blades down into Dodge's back. She was not strong enough to drive them very deeply into the man, but it was enough to make Dodge pull back, roaring with pain. As he did so, the scissors flew from Helen's grasp.

Freed of his bulk, she jumped to her feet. Dodge pushed himself erect and came for her, furious. She jumped aside nimbly, but when she turned to run, she tripped over a boulder in the darkness. As she sprawled face down, a lightning bolt slammed into the earth only yards away. At almost the same instant, a terrifying clap of thunder broke above her. She dug her fingers into the ground as a second bolt of lightning seared through the atmosphere, turning the night into day. In its eerie, livid light, she saw Sam Dodge lurching toward her.

More terrified of him than of the storm, Helen scrambled to her feet just as an ear-shattering peal of thunder ripped through the heavens. The sudden, torrential downpour that followed was like a single sheet of water emptied from a giant tub. Its impact almost beat her into the ground, but she kept on running, desperate to escape from Dodge.

As she ran, the lightning flashed almost continuously, and the thunder caused the ground beneath her feet to shift. Still Helen fled through the night, plunging blindly through the storm like a wild, terrified animal. She did not know if Sam Dodge was still chasing her. It no longer mattered. She ran instinctively, without thought, at the mercy of her terror.

Abruptly the ground beneath her feet opened up. Screaming, Helen plunged through space. Suddenly a rocky slope struck her, and she felt herself tumbling over and over into a numbing, blessed darkness. . . .

Chapter Seven

Less than a mile away from Helen and the stage robbers, Clint and John Ferris found the sudden cloudburst too violent for them to proceed. The visibility was so poor there was a danger their horses would stumble into a ravine and lose their footing—or worse.

Clint had to scramble to find a safe spot for their horses. He knew that in such a storm attaching hobbles to their legs could not be counted on to prevent the horses from drifting away, so they were tied to a stunted pine sheltered among some rocks. Then the two men made a wet, miserable camp against the side of a cliff, relying on an overhanging rock shelf to protect them from the driving rain.

Clint felt frustrated. He had been certain they would overtake Sutter and the gold within the hour. As he had planned it, in the darkness they would sneak up on the highwaymen's encampment, free Helen, then surprise and disarm Sutter and the other two. Before the night was over, Clint would have been well on his way to his father's ranch, leaving the actor with the highwaymen as his captives, the gold shipment and Helen both rescued, and Ferris a hero.

He glanced up at the sheets of rain thundering down out of the flickering sky and pulled his sopping jacket closer. Clint wished he had thought to pack his slicker. His Levi's were plastered to him as tightly as a second layer of skin, and an almost steady stream of water trickled off his hat. The rain even had forced its way into his boots, drenching his toes. Every seam in his clothing had been saturated. And though Clint had done his best to keep the firing chambers of his six-gun and Winchester dry, he knew he dared not trust his gunpowder.

Beside him, Ferris was sitting with his back to the rock face, his red velvet-lined cape wrapped around him like a blanket. He looked surprisingly serene. Clint had to admit that so far the actor had been able to keep up with him without complaint, even though it was obvious the fellow had not sat a horse in some time.

"This rain will delay us," Ferris remarked suddenly, "but it should not change the outcome, I imagine. Those three cannot really escape us. Not now. After this rain the ground will be soft and their tracks should be even easier to follow."

"If we find their tracks again," Clint reminded him. "We may lose them completely in these badlands."

Ferris glanced sharply at Clint. "Is that a real possibility?"

"Hell, yes."

The actor sighed wearily. "Well, wouldn't you say there's a good chance that—like us—they have been forced to stop and seek shelter?"

"Sounds likely," Clint conceded.

"Then we know they aren't still moving away from us. And there's some chance we will find their tracks when the rain stops."

"If it stops," Clint amended.

"But surely this is just a cloudburst," Ferris protested.

"If you know that, you know more than I do. This country has been needing a long, soaking rain for a month or so. It looks to me like this is it."

Ferris thought for a moment, then shrugged. "Still, these men are doomed."

Clint stirred irritably. "How the hell do you know that?"

"I know it, Clint, because they are men without imagination."

"What's that supposed to mean?" Clint snapped.

"Thieves are fools. All of them. They suffer from a defect of the imaginative faculty," Ferris said very matter of factly.

Though Clint could not help but be impressed by the actor's verbal facility, he was somewhat put off by the man's cocksureness. Lifting an eyebrow, he said, "Well, now, is that so? You have that on good authority, do you?"

Undaunted by his companion's tone, Ferris plunged on, warming to his topic. "Don't you see, Clint? Without the ability to imagine, those outlaws cannot see ahead." The man tapped his temple with a forefinger. "They cannot imagine what follows each action they take. Their robbery was doomed, therefore, from the very start. Take the matter of the stagecoach. Obviously, they did not foresee that it would plunge down into a ravine. That must have cost them valuable time. And remember, it was this miscalculation which allowed us to catch up to them."

Clint could offer no argument to that, and he leaned back to listen as the actor went on.

"In taking Helen," Ferris said, "they caused us to follow after them far more diligently than would otherwise have been the case. Furthermore, as soon as word gets out that they have kidnapped a woman and taken her hostage, the entire countryside will be after them. And what about Sam Dodge, the one you shot? Surely he will cause trouble for them."

"Okay. So they have trouble. But they've also got the gold and a head start," Clint argued. "And now they've got a cloudburst to cover their tracks. If they get over the mountains and reach California, they will have escaped for good."

Ferris was astonished. "Surely, Clint, you do not really believe that."

"Why the hell shouldn't I?"

The actor looked at Clint as if he were seeing him for the first time. "Perhaps you lack sufficient imagination as well, Clint. But consider this: a young girl packing a huge Colt revolver, an obviously unprincipled gun-toting male companion, and a wounded fat man in bad shape. Now imagine these three leading packhorses laden with freshly minted gold from the Denver mint. How could such a menagerie possibly escape notice?"

Unable to disagree with what the actor had said so far, Clint simply shrugged.

"Let's assume they go into hiding," Ferris went on. "How could they ever stay hidden? In order to survive, they will have to spend some of that freshly minted gold on supplies, a new horse, perhaps. If they move from their hiding place, they will have to camp somewhere. No matter where they go, they will leave traces. Inevitably, they must become a part of the world around them. Indeed, these three—as a result of their crime—are even now a moving light in a dark wood, impossible to miss. They will never escape detection and eventual capture.''

Clint was sobered. What Ferris said hit him with the force of a blow. Once he had allowed himself to listen, it occurred to him that the actor's unsettling conclusions were right on the mark. Sutter and his two sidekicks lacked the imagination to see what lay ahead of them once they robbed the stage.

But that same lamentable lack of imagination could just as easily be applied to Clint, as well. He had certainly never sat down and taken the time to think through the consequences of what he was doing when he first decided to go into the bank in Gunnison and demand a loan. And when he had taken out his Colt, he had done so without considering for a moment what lay beyond that fateful action. Like the outlaws he now pursued, Clint had allowed himself to see only the money and his need for it.

Clint shook his head and took a deep breath. Now here he was, hunkered down in the rain like a drenched rat, pursuing three outlaws in the company of a dude from the East because of his concern for a kidnapped woman he barely knew. Yet, if he had had any sense—any imagination, as Ferris would say—he must see that in continuing after Sutter, Clint might be dooming both himself and his father.

The actor glanced at Clint, obviously wondering at his silence. Ferris cleared his throat. "I guess perhaps all that talk about imagination might seem presumptuous of me," he remarked, smiling ruefully at his companion. "After all, what does a fellow like me know? I'm just an actor. The real world and those who inhabit it are strange and unfamiliar to me. You must forgive my pontifications,

Clint. I got carried away. This is your world. You know it and the people who inhabit it far better than I do.''

"Don't be so sure of that, actor," Clint said, staring gloomily out at the rain.

Ferris seemed mollified somewhat. He relaxed and looked with concern at Clint. "Tell me, won't this business take you out of your way?"

"It might."

"I suppose you have family, friends waiting for you. Will your delay trouble them?"

"There's no one waiting for me," Clint said quietly.

Ferris persisted. "You mean you were just riding by when you heard that shot?"

"Where I might be going and where I come from are none of your business," Clint snapped.

"Oh."

Clint turned to stare at Ferris. "I'm warning you now, actor, you'd better not ask any more men you meet out here those kinds of questions. It's very impolite—dangerous even."

"I see." Ferris leaned back against the cliff face and wrapped his cloak more tightly about himself. He had been reprimanded and knew it.

Clint flicked the collar of his jacket about his neck, hunched down, and folded his arms. He was no longer interested in conversing with the actor. The fellow had already given him too damn much to think on.

Besides, during the last few minutes, the thunder had risen to a hellish crescendo, effectively stopping any conversation. A series of shattering detonations tore away at the ground under their feet. The wind's cry rose to a demented pitch. Peering bleakly out from under their meager shelter, Clint caught sight of the lashing curtains of rain, gleaming in the nearly continuous flashes of lightning.

He pushed himself farther back against the cliff face. But it was no use. The stinging rain swept in under the rock, drenching both men. The miserable night threatened to get even worse before daylight.

In the shallow cave where he had taken refuge, Carl Sutter shook Lorna May insistently. Despite the fury of the storm, she had fallen fast asleep. She was one hell of a woman, Sutter realized, as he watched her stir drowsily and sit up. She would pleasure a man in broad daylight with all the world watching and then sleep through an earthquake.

Staring blearily at him, Lorna May ran a hand through her tangled hair. "What is it, Carl? I just got to sleep."

"This here rain! It's just what we need," he told her. "If them two is trackin' us, there ain't no way they can follow us in this. I'll bet they're holin' up in that canyon back there right this minute. The thing for us to do is move out—now!"

"In the middle of this storm?" she asked incredulously.

"Why not? This here rain'll wipe out any tracks we leave, and no one ever died from being rained on. We're near the end of the badlands now. There's a valley not too far ahead of us, and the mountains just beyond that."

Lorna May stared out at the rain. It caused a steady, deafening roar as it pounded down upon the rocks and hard ground. "We better keep to high ground, if we do move out," she pointed out. "Them gullies will be flooding soon, and that water'll be heavy and mean."

"Hell, I know that, Lorna May. I seen flash floods before. Like you say, we'll keep to the high ground."

"What about Sam? He's hurt bad, and he ain't in no mood to do much—not with that schoolteacher gone."

"We leave him."

"Suppose he don't want to stay behind?" Lorna May asked.

Sutter smiled and patted the grips of his six-gun. "This here'll convince him."

For Lorna May, that seemed to be enough. She brightened and threw back her slicker. "I'll go get the horses," she told Sutter, standing up. "You go see to Sam."

Sutter found Sam Dodge wrapped in his slicker under some pines on the slope above the cave. His horse was tied to a sapling beside him.

Taking out his weapon, Sutter reached in under the low pine boughs and poked Dodge in the shoulder with his gun barrel. He was not gentle. But Dodge did not stir. Perhaps he was already dead, Sutter thought as he nudged the man one more time. There was still no response from the big man. He lay there, a large, sodden mass of flesh.

Sutter pulled back and straightened up. Hell—no sense in trying to wake the slob up. If he was not dead yet, he soon would be. Sutter might as well save himself a bullet. Sutter holstered his gun, turned, and started back down the slope.

"Hey!" Dodge cried from behind him.

Sutter spun. Standing like a disheveled bear on the slope above him was Dodge. He was holding his left arm up to ward off the driving rain as he peered down at Sutter.

"Was that you just pokin' me?" the fat man asked.

"Yes, it was, Sam."

"What's up?" Dodge asked.

118

"We're going," Sutter said, his hand falling to the grips of his revolver.

"In this? I'm gettin' worse, Carl. I'll need help!" Dodge protested.

"No. This is our chance. We're moving out."

Dodge saw that Sutter was not to be dissuaded. He shrugged wearily. "All right. I'll saddle up. But you've got to help me."

"No need for that!" Sutter shouted above the storm as he lifted his weapon from its holster. The distance between the two men was not quite ten yards. Aiming casually, Sutter pulled the trigger.

The gun misfired.

With a howl of rage, Dodge flung himself down the slope at Sutter.

Sutter thumbcocked the revolver just as Dodge hit him. Both men crashed to the ground, Dodge on top. Sutter squeezed the trigger again. This time the gun fired, the explosion muffled by Dodge's bulk. The bullet caught him in the right side. With a groan, the fat man rolled off Sutter and tumbled about ten feet farther down the slope, where he lay, face down, the rain pounding his head into the sodden slope.

Getting to his feet, Sutter did his best to wipe off the mud that clung to him from head to foot. He picked up his hat, emptied it out, and clapped it back onto his soaking head, then went down to inspect Sam Dodge. Halting beside him, Sutter waited warily for the fat man to stir, his gun cocked and waiting. When Dodge did not move, Sutter kicked him viciously in the side, at the point where the bullet had gone in. Sutter thought he glimpsed a dark flood pouring from the wound.

Satisfied, Sutter hurried to join Lorna May, his back hunched against the driving, punishing rain.

Despite the fearsome thunder that had kept the children awake and the relentless pounding of the rain, Annie Foster had almost dropped off to sleep when she heard the pounding come again.

She sat up, her heart thudding in her throat. There was no denying it this time. It was not the storm. Someone was pounding on her door! But who could it possibly be at such an hour?

The pounding resumed, louder than before. In a panic, she flung back her bedclothes, grabbed her bathrobe, and stepped into her slippers. Hurrying into the kitchen, she crossed to the heavy door and placed her ear against it.

"Who is it?" she cried. "Who's out there?"

"Lone Bear!" came the reply.

Astonished, Annie slipped the bolt back and pulled open the door. Lone Bear strode into the kitchen, a portion of the storm entering with him. Soaked to the skin, he was carrying someone wrapped in his saddle blanket. Peering at the face, which was fearfully scratched and bloodied, Annie realized that Lone Bear was carrying a white woman.

Stepping back, she said quickly, "Take her into my bedroom, Lone Bear. Quickly. It's down that hallway."

With a brisk nod, Lone Bear carried the woman down the short hall into the bedroom, Annie close behind. As Annie lit a lamp on her dresser, the big Indian put his burden down gently on the bed, then stood back.

Annie lifted the blanket off the woman and examined her. Though it appeared the woman had no serious injuries or broken bones, Annie was concerned at what she saw. The woman's legs and knees were battered fearfully, and there were several lacerations on her head and a sharp cut under one ear. Annie judged the woman to be in her early twenties. She appeared taller than most women and, despite her battered features, decidedly beautiful, with long, auburn hair, arching brows, and a full, expressive mouth.

"Ma! Who's that?" Ephraim asked.

Startled, Annie turned to see Ephraim and Marylou standing in their nightgowns in her bedroom doorway. Marylou had her hand in Ephraim's. Both were watching her wide-eyed.

"Go to the kitchen, children, and wait for me," Annie told them. "Ephraim, can you put some fresh kindling in the stove?"

The boy nodded quickly.

"Do it then."

Ephraim and Marylou vanished.

Annie turned to Lone Bear. "What happened to this woman? Where did you find her?"

"She came through the badlands with three other whites. These whites are bad medicine, for sure. Their packhorses carry very heavy load. It is gold, I think. They are mad for it, like all whites."

"Did they do this to her?" Annie asked, furious at the thought.

"I watched them as they come near valley. They made camp, and she flee from one of them. The storm broke then. She run like crazy woman, without sense, and disappear near cliff. So I search for her and find her near bottom of the slope. She is alive, all right. But I think she need to be cared for."

Annie nodded briskly. "I'll get some hot water and bandages and wash off her wounds. Thank you for bringing her, Lone Bear. I am sure you did the right thing."

He smiled. "I know you would take care of her. I will go the kitchen and help Ephraim build fire in stove."

"Thank you, Lone Bear."

As Lone Bear left the room, Annie turned back to her patient. As she did so, the woman stirred fitfully. Annie leaned close as the woman's eyelids fluttered, then opened. Turning her head, the woman saw Annie leaning over her.

Resting a comforting hand on the woman's shoulder, Annie said, "You'll be safe here. Lie still and rest."

"Where is this place? The last time I remember I was in the storm running—!" Panic began to seize the woman as her memory returned.

"Lone Bear found you and brought you here," Annie reassured her. "I'll explain later. Just lie still now. You took a very bad fall."

"Yes! Now I remember." She shuddered from head to foot. "I'm so . . . sore!" Then she looked fearfully beyond Annie. "Are you sure they haven't followed me here?"

"Who's they?" Annie asked.

"Sam Dodge and the others! They robbed the stage and took me hostage!"

"Don't worry about them now," Annie insisted, patting the woman's hand. "I am sure Lone Bear did not lead them here. Not in this storm, surely. You're safe now."

The woman took a deep breath and appeared to relax a bit. Holding up her arms and looking down at her dress, she uttered a tiny cry of dismay. "I'm filthy," she said. "I'll ruin your bed!"

"Now, don't bother about that," Annie said with a smile. "My name is Annie Foster. What's yours?"

"Helen. Helen Bromfield."

"I am pleased to meet you, Helen. It would have

been nicer if we could have met under pleasanter circumstances. Now, you just lie still. I'll be back to tend to your wounds. Are you hungry?''

"Not now," Helen said wearily. "I'm just tired—and sore.''

As Annie stepped back, Helen closed her eyes and appeared to sink at once into a deep, restful sleep. Relieved, Annie hurried from the bedroom.

An hour or so later, Annie had managed to clean the mud and dried blood off Helen's face and body. What Annie found was encouraging. There were many cuts, but for the most part they were only skin-deep, and though the bruises were not pleasant to look at, Annie was sure Helen would recover nicely.

She dressed the groggy woman in her own nightgown, then tucked her snuggly under the covers and returned to the kitchen. She found that her two children had long since gone to bed, leaving Lone Bear asleep at the table, his head resting on his folded arms. Annie shook Lone Bear gently.

The big Indian awoke at once and sat up.

"Thanks for your help, Lone Bear," she told him. "I think Helen is going to be just fine. There were no serious injuries. That terrible fall she took didn't help her any, but I'm sure she'll survive.''

Lone Bear got to his feet and nodded solemnly. "These white men who take her from the stagecoach. They bring death with them, I think. You must be careful.''

"I will. You can be sure of that, Lone Bear.''

He walked to the door and opened it. A blast of rain-laden wind caused Annie to take a step back. The light from the lamp on the table caught the gleaming ropes of rain still pouring out of the black heavens.

"Good night, Lone Bear."

"Good night, Annie Foster."

Ducking his head, Lone Bear walked out into the rain. A bolt of lightning momentarily illuminated his striding figure. Though the rain sweeping through the doorway was drenching the skirts of her nightgown, Annie continued to watch Lone Bear until he disappeared. Then she pushed shut the door—and bolted it.

Chapter Eight

Sam Dodge was not dead yet.

The moment he felt Carl Sutter's bullet rip into his side, he realized he was at a serious disadvantage and allowed himself to tumble past Sutter and on down the slope. Lying face down in the mud, he heard Sutter approach and waited tensely as Sutter stood over him. At any moment he expected to hear Sutter thumbcock his Colt. Dodge realized his only hope was that Sutter would think him already dead. When Sutter kicked him in the side, a feeble groan escaped his lips, but the rain drowned out its sound.

After Sutter moved off, Dodge remained on the slope, fearful that Sutter might return. Meanwhile, Dodge's senses were reeling, and despite the rain pounding him relentlessly, a furnacelike heat was burning his body. He was just about ready to get to his feet and make a run for it when he heard Lorna May approaching with Sutter to inspect what they both thought was a corpse. Lorna May poked Dodge judiciously with her foot, then stepped back. They might have been inspecting a newly dressed side of beef. Over the intermittent thunder and driving rain, Dodge had difficulty hearing what Lorna May was saying to Sutter. But as they turned and walked away, Dodge heard the young woman's laugh clearly enough.

For an interminable time, Dodge waited for them to pull out. When they did at last, Dodge was so weak he could barely lift his head to watch them go. Only when the shifting curtains of rain finally closed behind them and the three packhorses they were leading did he push himself off the ground and stagger to his feet. The wound in Dodge's side was burning like a branding iron, while the hot blood from it ran down his leg. Turning, he struggled back up the slope, found his hat, and after considerable effort managed to saddle and mount his horse.

He had not followed Sutter and Lorna May very far before he realized he would have to do something about the wound in his side. It continued to bleed profusely, and Dodge was getting weaker by the minute. Pulling his horse to a halt, he worked his gunbelt higher on his waist, then snugged it tighter around the wound. The pain that followed made him groan aloud. The world tipped dizzily, and Dodge felt himself about to topple backward from his saddle. Reaching out with his left hand, he grabbed the saddle horn and clung to it grimly. The dizziness finally passed, leaving him somewhat light-headed—giddy, even. Awkwardly, since he could use only his left hand, he pulled the brim of his hat down to protect the back of his neck from the rain, then urged his horse on after Sutter and Lorna May. Dodge was driven by only one desire—to catch up to those two sons of bitches and blow them out of their saddles.

It wasn't long before he glimpsed Sutter, Lorna May,

and the three packhorses going down the narrow trail leading from the badlands to the valley floor. The thunder and lightning had moved on, but steady, solid sheets of rain continued to fall. The world had become a gray, sodden land of pools, rivulets, and mud. Exhausted, his teeth chattering persistently, Dodge booted his mount to a halfhearted lope.

By the time he reached the trail they had taken down through the rocks, Sutter and Lorna May were riding across the valley floor below him, heading for the mountains only dimly visible on its far side. Dodge rode as far as he could into the rimrocks, but one glance at the steep trail told him he could not follow them any farther. And if he did not act fast, they would escape for good.

Slipping off his horse, Dodge snaked his rifle from its scabbard and lurched toward a low boulder that gave him an unobstructed view of the valley below. The steady rain made judging distance difficult, but he estimated Sutter and Lorna May to be less than two hundred yards away, still within range of his Sharps.

Dodge had some difficulty aiming the rifle. He could not tuck the stock into his right shoulder, and when he tucked it against his left shoulder, he could barely hold the rifle steady because of the earlier gunshot wound. But he had no choice in the matter, not if he wanted to bring down the two bastards. Gritting his teeth, he sighted down the long barrel and forced his right hand to hold the rifle steady. The pain in his arm made his head swim, but he concentrated grimly, and when the rifle's sights rested finally on Carl Sutter's back, Dodge pulled the trigger.

The Sharps' recoil caused a sharp, agonizing pain to knife through his right shoulder. He staggered back and almost fell, but caught himself in time. Dodge pushed himself back to the boulder and looked down. Sutter and Lorna May, untouched, had lifted their mounts to a lope. Cursing, Dodge aimed his rifle a second time and fired. This time he clung to the boulder and watched to see if he struck either of his targets.

A packhorse stumbled and went down.

"Damn!" he muttered, watching the fleeing outlaws continue to ride across the valley, the two remaining packhorses barely keeping up.

Dodge realized his targets were out of range. He sagged to the ground, his head whirling. For a moment he sat in the pounding rain, then, using his Sharps as a crutch, he pulled himself upright and started back through the rocks toward his horse.

Less than six feet from the animal, the Sharps slipped from Dodge's grasp, and he collapsed into the mud. He lifted his head once, then lay still. His horse had looked up at Dodge's approach, then it lowered its head and resumed cropping the grass at its feet. As it fed, it began to drift back up to the trail.

Sutter pulled up and looked back in the direction of the rifle shots. Lorna reined in also and turned her horse as the rain beat down steadily.

"That was Sam," Sutter said.

"I figured."

"Dammit! I thought I killed him," Sutter swore.

Lorna May said nothing.

"He's finished now," Sutter said hopefully, hunching forward against the wind and rain. A steady rivulet poured off his hat brim. "He would've kept on firing if he wasn't."

"We're out of range. That's why he stopped," Lorna May pointed out.

"Not with that Sharps, we ain't. A man ain't hardly ever out of range of that rifle."

Lorna May sat her horse stolidly and peered through the rain at Sutter like a cat sizing up a new master.

"I say we go back and get that gold," Sutter told her.

"You sure that's such a good idea?"

"You want to leave all that gold?" Sutter was aghast at the thought.

"No," she said. "I don't."

"Let's go, then."

Pulling the remaining packhorses with them, they rode back to the fallen horse. Dismounting swiftly, they ignored the dying horse's thrashing and proceeded to transfer the gold to the other packhorses. As they worked, they were both conscious of the rocks looming over them and the fact that if Dodge were not dead, he might open up on them again at any moment. They worked swiftly and wordlessly.

Soon they were back in their saddles, leading the two remaining packhorses across the valley floor. In the soft, muddy grassland, the heavily laden horses began to founder. Sutter and Lorna May pulled them on ruthlessly, heading toward a river emerging from the shifting curtains of rain that continued to drum down upon them.

Clint Dennison and John Ferris had moved out before dawn. They were too wet to sleep and too bored to remain where they were any longer. Since Sutter had been heading due west, Clint continued in that direction. Pushing on as swiftly as he could, Clint was well aware that the continuing rain had washed out the tracks he had been following the day before. All he could hope for was to find where Sutter had camped during the night. There he would find new tracks, deep impressions in the soggy ground. In the driving rain they would not last long. Clint was becoming discouraged when he heard a shot echo dimly through the drizzle.

"Where'd that come from?" Ferris asked eagerly, looking about him. "Which direction?"

"Shut up and listen," Clint ordered.

A moment later there was a second shot. This time, Clint was sure the sound had come from his right. He waited a moment longer. When there were no more shots, he pulled his mount around and started across a small, sodden clearing, heading toward a dim outline of rocks beyond it. Ferris was close behind.

Before Clint reached the rocks, he turned onto a trail leading to the north. About a hundred yards farther on, he came upon a saddled horse cropping grass alongside the trail. Clint dismounted and examined both horse and saddle. Despite the driving rain there were still traces of blood on the right skirts, and the rifle scabbard was empty. He looked around. The drenched ground alongside the trail was clearly marked by the horse's hooves. Following the hoofprints, Clint found himself close to a ridge overlooking a valley. He followed the ridge and found heavy, lurching bootprints gouged out of the soft ground.

"We're getting lucky," he called back to Ferris, who was still astride his horse.

As Ferris dismounted, Clint followed the footprints around a large boulder and almost stumbled over Sam Dodge's sodden body. Clint approached the still body cautiously.

"That's one of them!" Ferris exclaimed, coming up from behind Clint. "That's Dodge!"

There was a Sharps rifle beside the body. Clint bent and picked it up. The rifle's muzzle was clogged with mud and the breech was drenched, but Clint could still smell a trace of recently fired gunpowder. There was no doubt about it. Dodge had fired the two shots they had heard.

Looking down at Dodge, Clint nudged the big fellow in the side with the tip of his boot and frowned. He thought he heard a groan, but it was difficult to tell with the pelting rain. He hunkered down beside the fat man and shook his shoulder. Suddenly Sam Dodge rolled over, a smile on his mud-splattered face and a huge Colt in his left hand.

As Dodge's finger tightened about the trigger, John Ferris swiftly stepped forward and kicked the revolver out of Dodge's hand. The gun detonated as it went, the bullet narrowly missing Clint's cheek. Jumping up, Clint drew his own revolver and aimed it at the fat man.

Dodge stared up expressionlessly. "I'm dead already," he said, his voice barely audible. "I got two rounds in me. Go ahead. Shoot me. Make it quicker. I'd sure appreciate it."

Clint holstered his weapon and turned to Ferris. "Thanks," he said. "The sonofabitch caught me by surprise."

"Now we're even, Clint," Ferris said.

Clint nodded and looked back down at Dodge. The man was still staring up at them, but the rain was pelting glazed eyes.

Ferris peered closely at Dodge. "He's really dead this time," he said.

"I hope so."

Clint looked around, wondering which way the others had gone—and who Dodge had been shooting at. Suddenly he heard the clash of hooves on rock from behind. He whirled and saw two riders approaching, one of them considerably younger than the other.

As the men rode up, Clint's heart fell. The older rider was wearing a star, as was his deputy. There was no doubt in Clint's mind where the two men were from and who they were after. For just a moment he thought of going for his gun, but he held himself in check. A better time would come, he told himself as he looked into the approaching sheriff's cool, steady eyes.

Chapter Nine

Carl Sutter yanked hard and swore. The packhorse stumbled, regained its balance, then went down, as if the muddy ground were swallowing it up. The foundering horse lifted its head frantically and tried to get up. For a moment it seemed as if it were trying to drink the light rain that continued to fall. Then it gave up and lay down on its side, its forelegs pawing feebly.

Lorna May did not dismount. She dropped the reins of the packhorse she was leading, turned her horse, and rode over to look down at the dying animal. Sutter had dismounted the moment the packhorse began to founder. He strode angrily to the dying horse and looked at it furiously. It obviously was finished.

"I told you we were going too fast," Lorna May said. "I told you we better give it a rest."

Sutter glanced up at her. "Shut up!" he snapped. "I don't need you to tell me how to lead a packhorse."

Lorna May steadied her horse with a gentle pat to its neck. "Maybe you do, Carl. These horses are overloaded and the going is pretty damn heavy in this mud. It's like riding through molasses.''

"Cut it out, will you?'' he snarled. "What the hell choice do we have?''

"From now on, I say we go slower,'' Lorna May insisted, a tight smile on her face. She had decided that if Sutter struck her, she would draw her revolver and shoot the sonofabitch in the face.

Sutter saw the steel in her eyes and decided to back off. "Okay,'' he said. "Okay. So I pushed the horse too hard. What do we do now?''

"Lighten the horses. They're both carrying too much,'' Lorna May suggested.

"You mean leave some of this gold behind?''

The girl nodded. "Yes. Bury it. Along the riverbank over there. We can come back for it later.''

"I don't like it. We might never get back here,'' Sutter protested.

"Well, then, you can carry it yourself. On your horse. Put this gold in your saddlebags.''

"Then I'd lose my own horse,'' Sutter pointed out.

"Well, then, bury it here, for Christ's sake—or leave it.''

"All right,'' Sutter said. "All right. I think you're crazy. But we'll do what you say. Bury it for now.''

Lorna May dismounted. "Unstrap the bags. I'll find a spot along the river to bury them.''

While Sutter set to work unstrapping the bags, Lorna May headed to the riverbank about twenty-five yards away. As she walked, she realized how difficult it must have been for the packhorses to walk in the mud. The heels of her boots sank deeply into the saturated meadowland, making a loud, sucking noise each time she pulled them free.

The river was swollen from the rain, but much of the bank was still above the water. She worked her way carefully down the steep embankment, looking for a likely spot to bury the gold. She had just about settled on a deep cut in the bank when the clouds above her broke apart momentarily. A small patch of blue appeared, and a shaft of sunlight brightened the river. Glancing up, Lorna May saw a ranch house and two outbuildings tucked snuggly into a bend in the river a mile or so farther along. As she stared at the scene, the clouds closed in again, and the ranch was swallowed up in the rain.

She clambered back up the embankment and hurried across the meadowland to Sutter. When she reached him, he was pulling free of the downed horse the aparejo in which the loose coins had been packed.

"We don't have to bury the gold," she told Sutter, panting slightly.

He glanced up at her. "What the hell do you mean?"

"There's a ranch about a mile or so down the river. If we just keep going, maybe we can get fresh mounts. We can either buy them or just take them."

Sutter scrambled to his feet. "A ranch out here? Where?"

She pointed. "You can't see it from here. But I saw it when the rain let up. It's on the other side of them willows, about a mile down the river."

Sutter nodded happily. "Well, that's better!" he said, grinning. "Here. Help me lug this gold over to my horse. He can carry it that far, anyway. Then we'll just help ourselves to fresh mounts. And this here rain is finally letting up. Our troubles are over."

Lorna May did not say anything as she bent to help Sutter lift the gold-filled packsaddle. She hoped he was right, but so far nothing about this job had gone right, and she was beginning to wonder if anything would.

At the Foster ranch Helen Bromfield lay awake in bed, listening to the sounds of activity coming from the kitchen. The noises comforted and warmed her. Though she was still sore all over, the breakfast Annie Foster had brought her and the eagerness of the two children as they helped had filled Helen with such a feeling of gratitude and contentment that she had been moved almost to tears.

These were the hardworking, plain people she had so detested as she observed them during her trip west. Helen had considered them drab, without color or life, miserable people inhabiting a lonely, unfriendly world. Yet, had she been miraculously returned to the bosom of her family in Boston, she could not have been treated with more consideration or patience—or love.

An Indian brought me here! Helen suddenly remembered. According to Annie, he was a Ute called Lone Bear, and he had seen Helen running from Dodge. He had followed her through the rain and then carried her on his horse all the way to the Foster ranch. As Helen went over it in her mind, she visualized with a shudder what a soaked, bedraggled mess she must have been when she arrived in the dead of the night. Yet Annie had given up her own bed to Helen, bathed her, and then dressed her in a nightgown. And though Helen could not be absolutely certain, it seemed that once or twice during the night she had awakened to see Annie sitting in anxious vigil by her bed.

Helen moved her legs under the covers, luxuriating in

the feel of the clean sheets. She was free at last of that filthy fat man and that shameless, gun-toting hussy and her lover. The more she thought of them, the more appalled she became. It was Lorna May who filled her with the most disgust. That girl-woman had exhibited a depravity so flagrant and unashamed that it stunned Helen. To see a woman so lacking in scruples, so cold-blooded, had been a terrible revelation. For it meant a person's gender had no bearing on behavior, that men and women were alike in their capacity for evil—and for good.

Helen had fled Boston nourishing a mistrust of all males because of the actions of one weak cad. Now she saw clearly that to have reacted in such a way was the response of a foolish, unthinking child. How could she possibly judge all men by the actions of that silly Paul Washburn? Furthermore, how could she have allowed herself to be so devastated by such a man? How had losing him been anything but a blessing?

Suddenly Helen thought of John Ferris.

During her train ride from Denver and her short stay at the hotel in Gunnison, she had acted abominably toward him. Only when they reached the stage station had she relented a little. Alone in that dim, crude place, she had been grateful for his friendly, encouraging smile. And then she had begun to find out how wrong she had been about him. With John Ferris as a companion, she had laughed for the first time in months, truly enjoying the company of another human being.

During the holdup, Ferris had tried to protect her. Each time he had been clubbed brutally for his efforts. In fact, if an unknown rifleman had not shot the fat man, the actor would be dead—for trying to save her.

John Ferris had proved himself to be a true gentleman,

even risking his life for her. What did it matter that he was an actor? He had a fine sensitivity. Indeed, his profession simply meant that he was familiar with some of the greatest poetry ever written and could be an eloquent, entertaining companion. And since when was such an accomplishment anything but a recommendation?

Helen's parents had taught her to look down on actors and the world of the theater. And that milksop, Paul Washburn, who had broken his engagement to her, had been more her parents' choice for her husband than her own. Surely, there was an important lesson for her in all this, she thought. Since it was Helen who would have to live with any decisions made concerning her life, she decided to see to it that those decisions were made by her, not by someone else.

Helen sighed. There was very little likelihood that she would ever see John Ferris again. And that was too bad. She would have liked him to know how much she appreciated his kindness and his gallantry in attempting to save her from Sam Dodge and the others.

Helen glanced out the window. The rain was no longer drumming on the roof as insistently as it had been, and the world had become considerably brighter. Sitting up, she flung back her covers and got out of bed. She felt a little woozy at first, but that soon passed. Annie had left slippers and a robe for her by the bed, and Helen put them on. The homey sounds coming from the kitchen pulled her in that direction.

Young Ephraim was just entering the kitchen from the porch carrying an armload of kindling for the great black iron stove squatting in the corner. He stopped when he saw Helen. Marylou was sitting at the table, paring potatoes. She was so tiny her mother had piled books up onto the seat of the chair to get her high enough. The little girl had already filled half a bowl with sliced and pared potatoes, her tiny voice singing cheerfully as she worked. At the kitchen sink alongside the hand pump, Annie was washing a recently plucked chicken.

"Helen!" cried Annie, as she caught sight of the woman standing in the doorway. "What are you doing out of bed? You need to rest."

"I'm fine," Helen insisted with a smile, walking into the kitchen. "Please. Don't mind me. Just go ahead about your work. Perhaps I could help some."

"Now, there's no need to think of that," Annie said, wiping her hands with a towel and hurrying toward Helen. "You've been through a terrible ordeal. Here, sit down beside Marylou."

As Helen sat down, Ephraim kicked the door shut behind him and marched over to the woodbin beside the stove and dumped the kindling into it.

"Is it still raining?" Helen asked him.

He blushed furiously. "It's let up some," he said.

"We'll need more wood, Ephraim," Annie told the boy.

Nodding obediently, Ephraim hurried from the kitchen.

"He's such a help," Annie said, sitting down beside Helen. "You have no idea. And of course he's all excited by your dramatic appearance. He asked this morning if you could stay with us."

Helen blushed with pleasure. "You've all been so kind. I'll never forget it."

"Nonsense!" Annie replied.

"Will you?" Marylou piped up, her eyes glowing. "Will you stay with us?"

"For a while," Helen assured Marylou, hugging her.

"But only if you let me help you peel some of those potatoes."

Marylou nodded eagerly and promptly gave Helen a potato.

With a laugh, Annie handed a paring knife to Helen. "I guess you would feel better with something to do, at that. But you were so fearfully worn down last night—and this morning, too."

"I'm much better now, thanks to you. I'm sore all over but it doesn't seem to matter. I know I'm among friends."

Annie smiled warmly. She was not beautiful, Helen decided, but she had something far more exciting than beauty, a vibrant, active intelligence. It glowed in her face and eyes with the warmth of sunlight.

As Helen began peeling the potato, she looked about the kitchen. "This is such a warm, cozy place. Do you live here all alone, Annie?"

"Since my husband died, yes."

"Oh, I'm sorry. When was that?" Helen asked.

"Two years ago. The cholera took him. Some settlers passed through the valley on their way to California and stayed with us for a while. James would not think of them going on at the time, the weather in the mountains was so bad. When they pushed on at last, they left us with the cholera. All of us got fearfully sick, but it was James the sickness took."

"That must have been terrible for you," Helen said sympathetically.

Annie smiled slightly, thinking about her husband. "He was always a frail, gentle man, but he was strong in so many ways. And he did so love the children. But sometimes I felt he was not up to living in the West. He

140

would much rather read a book or write a poem than chase some fool beef cattle across our range." She sighed and looked at her guest. "And you, what about you, Helen? Are you on your way to meet your husband?"

Helen blushed. "I am afraid not. I'm on my way to Cimarron to meet a school committee."

Annie looked closely at the other woman. "Just then I caught something in your eyes, young lady. If you don't want to tell me about it, you don't have to." She smiled. "But I am a good listener."

Helen laughed softly and picked up another potato to peel, surprised at how soothing the simple task was. "Oh, there was a man, sure enough. A cad, really. I was involved with him, I thought, and terribly hurt when he broke our engagement. So I came west. I was a fool."

"Maybe you were, maybe you weren't. The West needs teachers—and women. Whatever brought you, I, for one, am glad you came. Cimarron is not far away. Perhaps we can become friends."

Helen placed her hand on Annie's. "We already are, Annie."

Ephraim came in, his hat off, his light hair barely visible above the load he was carrying. He was obviously trying to impress Helen with how strong he was. She watched him stagger over to the woodbin and dump the freshly split wood into it.

"The next time, Ephraim, you don't need to bring in the whole woodpile," Annie said gently.

Ephraim swept a blond cowlick off his forehead and took a deep breath. His face was as red as a beet. "All right, Ma."

"But aren't you afraid? I mean to be out here all

alone?'' Helen asked as Ephraim went outside for another load of wood.

"We're not really alone," Annie said.

"What do you mean?"

"The Ute Indians. They look after us, you might say," Annie explained.

Helen frowned. "Oh, yes. You said it was an Indian who found me last night and brought me here."

"Yes. Lone Bear."

"And you're not afraid of them?" Helen asked.

"I'm more afraid of a white man than I am of an Indian. If you treat an Indian fairly, he will never betray you. You can't always say that of a white person."

Helen considered that for a moment. She had not known any Indians personally, and the accounts of Indian massacres she had read in the East gave her little comfort. However, what she knew of her own people did not give her much comfort, either. And if Lone Bear had not brought her to the ranch, Helen would still be out there somewhere, hurting, and perhaps being hunted by the fat man and the others. Just thinking of that possibility made her shudder involuntarily.

"I'll take your word for it, Annie," Helen said, picking up another potato, "but you can imagine what I've read about Indians in the East. Some call them God's natural children, others insist they are cruel savages who must be exterminated if the West is to be made safe for Christians."

Annie looked at Helen thoughtfully. "You usually find in people what you expect to find."

At that moment Ephraim burst into the kitchen. This time he was not carrying any wood. "Ma!" he cried. "Someone's coming!"

At almost the same instant Helen heard the sound of pounding footsteps. She looked out the open door and saw Carl Sutter and Lorna May, their guns drawn, running across the yard toward the open door. Before she could jump up and slam it shut, Sutter had burst into the kitchen, Lorna May on his heels.

The terrifying suddenness of their entry terrified Marylou, and she burst into tears. At once Annie snatched her from the chair and held her securely in her arms. Ephraim, his eyes wide, found refuge at his mother's side.

Swiftly, Helen placed herself between Sutter and Annie.

"Don't harm these people," she said. "Please! I'll go with you. There's no need to cause them any trouble."

Sutter laughed at her. "Hell! It ain't you we want. It's horses. Fresh horses."

"Take them then," said Annie, "and get out."

"Sure. We'll do that. How many do you have?" Sutter asked.

"Six. But one mare is with foal," Annie replied.

"We'll take them all. It'll keep you from riding out to spread the word we was here."

"But we need horses. You must at least leave us a team. We are miles from stores and towns. We'll be stranded," Annie protested.

"That ain't our worry." Sutter laughed cruelly as he looked around the kitchen. He spotted the food cabinet that covered one complete wall.

"We need provisions," he told Lorna May. "Get over there and take what we need. I'll get some saddlebags."

He disappeared out the door. Annie and Helen stepped to one side with the children as Lorna May opened the food cabinet and began looting the shelves. Annie had already put up a winter's store of preserves and had purchased many canned goods as well. Sutter returned with two saddlebags, and Lorna May began stuffing them.

Helen could see the dismay on Annie's face as her provisions disappeared into the bags. Not satisfied with filling the two saddlebags he had just brought, Sutter went back for more. When he returned and tossed them to Lorna May, Annie stepped forward angrily.

"You can't take any more," she told Sutter. "You've taken enough. Without horses, we'll be unable to get new provisions, and now you are taking all that we have put aside. I have two children to feed!"

Sutter walked over to Annie and slapped her hard, sending her reeling backward.

"You can't hurt my Ma!" Ephraim cried, incensed.

Helen reached down to stop him, but the boy was too quick. Darting past her, he bowled into Sutter so fiercely that it knocked the man into the table, skidding it back into the kitchen sink. As Sutter fell heavily against it, the table collapsed, and he landed on the floor, surrounded by pieces of the table.

Sutter struggled up from the floor, but Ephraim continued to flail him. Helen rushed over to pull Ephraim away, but Lorna May got to the boy first. She grabbed Ephraim by the hair, hauled him upright, then flung him violently across the kitchen. The boy crashed into the wall, narrowly missing the stove. Dazed, he sagged to the floor.

Picking himself up, the furious Sutter drew his revolver and cocked it. "I'll kill the little bastard!" he cried, brandishing the gun. "I'll blow his brains out!"

Annie screamed as Sutter took careful aim at the stunned boy.

All at once a powerful, broad-chested Indian appeared in the open doorway. Startled, Sutter stepped back and swung his weapon in that direction. Ignoring the revolver, the Indian advanced menacingly on Sutter.

"Get back!" Sutter cried. "Get back you crazy Indian or I'll kill you!"

"Lone Bear!" Annie cried out. "Stop! He means it! He'll shoot!"

But Lone Bear did not pause. His face a cold mask of fury, he reached out for the weapon in Sutter's hand. Sutter ducked to one side and fired point-blank at the oncoming Indian. The bullet appeared to have found its mark as Lone Bear shuddered slightly, then steadied himself. But before Sutter could thumbcock his weapon and fire a second time, Lone Bear sprang at Sutter and tore the weapon from his grasp. Then, with a powerful blow, he knocked Sutter to the floor.

Lorna May drew her own gun. But before she could fire, Helen reached back, snatched up a cast-iron skillet, and brought it down as hard as she could on Lorna May's head. The frying pan thudded hollowly. Lorna May's knees gave out, and the gun in her hand dropped to the floor. She followed it, sprawling face down, unconscious.

Helen snatched up Lorna May's revolver. She was astonished at how heavy it was. Holding it with both hands, she managed to cock the weapon. In front of her, Lone Bear was sagging to the floor and Carl Sutter was scrambling to his feet. Helen quickly aimed at Sutter, closed her eyes, and pulled the trigger. The weapon detonated with a roar, its recoil pushing the gun violently upward. Helen hung on to it and opened her eyes. Carl Sutter was racing across the muddy yard.

She followed him and managed to cock the weapon a second time. Holding it more firmly, she fired at Sutter as he jumped onto a horse and spurred it frantically out of the yard. Before she could cock the weapon a third time, he had disappeared beyond the barn, the hoofbeats fading slowly into the distance.

Helen turned and walked back inside, the gun hanging heavily in her hand.

Chapter Ten

Sheriff Rex Barney was a chastened man. That morning he had been ready to quit, but it was Tim who had convinced him to keep on, despite the continuing rain and the lack of any tracks to follow. Then had come the distant rattle of two rifle shots. And it was his deputy who had heard the first one. Turning to the southwest, they headed in the direction from which Tim judged the shots had come.

They had kept on doggedly through the rain, and it looked like Tim had been right on target. Before them was the bank robber they were looking for, and he was standing over a dead man. Beside him stood a shorter, slighter man wearing a filthy cape, a narrow-brimmed hat, and mud-splattered spats. Rex decided it must be the actor the stationmaster had mentioned.

As the sheriff rode closer, his hand resting lightly on his revolver, he caught the dangerous, wary look that sprang into the tall fellow's eyes the moment he glimpsed the star on Rex's chest.

"You were right, Rex," Tim said softly, his own right hand dropping to his gun. "The bank robber and that dude are riding together."

Rex nodded. "Don't say anything, Tim. Stay back here and cover me. I'll handle this."

"Sure, Rex."

The sheriff rode closer to the two men, then pulled up and leaned casually over his pommel. The rain had let up a bit, but occasional wet gusts swept across his face. "Thought we heard rifle fire," he said. "What happened here?"

"Who're you?" the tall man asked.

"Sheriff Rex Barney from Gunnison. And that's my deputy back there."

"Our stage was held up, sheriff!" the dude said excitedly, "and this dead man here is one of the highwaymen!"

"Nice work," Rex replied, glancing over at the body of the man he reckoned to be Sam Dodge. "Are you two responsible for bringing this fellow down?"

"Maybe," said the tall man, stepping closer. "I put one bullet in him a while back, but I doubt if that was the fatal round."

Nodding, Rex dismounted. "I knew about the holdup," he said.

The bank robber accepted Rex's statement without comment. "They took a woman passenger hostage," he said. "We're hoping to overtake them and free her."

"Yes, I figured she'd been taken hostage when she was not left at the scene," Rex replied. He turned to the dude. "I assume you were her fellow passenger."

"I was. Allow me to introduce myself. I am John Ferris." The two men shook hands. "And this here is Clint. He saved my life. During the holdup, the fat man

148

was about to murder me when a timely round from Clint's rifle stopped him.''

"Clint, is it?'' Rex asked, turning to shake the bank robber's hand.

As he did so, he studied the man closely. Oppenheimer had described the bank robber perfectly, as had the stationmaster—a tall, square-shouldered fellow, clean-shaven, with a shock of dark-brown hair, thick eyebrows, a solid chin, and keen brown eyes.

There was only one thing wrong. The man did not have the look of an outlaw. Perhaps it was the honest, uncompromising light in his eyes or maybe the calm, erect way he held himself. And so far, according to Ferris's account and the sheriff's own observations, the bank robber had sure as hell not been acting like an outlaw.

"How'd you learn about the stage holdup, sheriff?'' Clint asked.

"Tim and I were tracking a bank robber. Sonofabitch robbed the bank in Gunnison. Then we came to the cairn beside the stage road. It didn't take much figuring to realize there'd been a holdup and that the stage had been taken to get at that gold shipment I'd been hearing about.''

As Rex spoke of the bank robbery, he watched Clint's eyes. They did not flicker. The man was certainly cool enough.

"Sheriff, you've got to help us,'' the actor anxiously broke in. "We've got to save Helen.''

"That's the woman passenger's name?''

"Yes. Helen Bromfield. She's in danger, Sheriff. Terrible danger. We've got to overtake those two who have her and make them give her up.''

"That won't be so easy,'' Rex commented.

"Standing around here won't make it any easier!" Ferris snapped.

"You got a point," the sheriff admitted. "Any idea which way they went?"

"Across the valley below us," Clint suggested. "Once they get into those mountains on the other side, it'll be downhill all the way to California."

Rex turned to see Tim watching from his horse. His young deputy looked confused. He was obviously wondering why Rex had not already disarmed the bank robber and taken him prisoner.

"I'll have to discuss this with my deputy," Rex said, leaving the two men and striding over to Tim.

The young man leaned down from his horse. "What's the matter, Rex?" he whispered hoarsely. "You ain't even drawn your gun yet. Ain't you sure that's the man? It looks like him to me."

"Sure, he's the man we been tailing," Rex said. "But just sit tight. Right now it's Sutter and that girlfriend of his I want. They're holding that woman passenger hostage, and I keep remembering how MacDougal and Billy looked under them rocks. I want Sutter bad. Real bad. Don't worry. I won't lose our bank robber. Hell, it looks like he'll be giving us a hand."

"You mean we're throwin' in with an outlaw?" Tim asked, astonished.

"Don't cross me in this, Tim. I sure won't appreciate it if you do," the sheriff warned.

Tim sat back in his saddle. "Hell, Rex, you know I wouldn't cross you. I'll back your play—all the way." He sighed. "Just be careful, that's all."

The sheriff smiled at Tim and slapped his thigh. "Don't you worry. I'll be careful enough for both of us."

Rex returned to the actor and the outlaw. "Let's mount up," he said. "We'll see if we can pick up any tracks in the valley below."

Clint looked at the sheriff and nodded.

It was clear to Rex the bank robber knew what kind of game Rex was playing. Cat and mouse. The only problem was that Clint was pretty damn big for a mouse, Rex thought.

The two men went for their horses and mounted up. Before long they came to the horse Sam Dodge had shot, and shortly afterward they reached the second packhorse. It was Clint who first caught sight of it. Dismounting, the four men inspected the dead animal.

"No sign of any bullet holes," Clint said angrily as he examined the horse. "But look at the eyes and the lather on his flanks. The bastards just rode this animal into the ground."

Rex shared Clint's anger and indignation.

The rain had stopped completely, and the tracks left by the outlaws' horses were stamped deeply into the soft, muddy turf. Rex realized they had only one packhorse left. That should sure as hell slow them down some, he thought.

The sheriff's party started up again, keeping parallel to the river. Before long they saw a dim line of willows materializing out of the still misty meadowland ahead of them.

Suddenly the peace was broken by dim, barely audible gunshots. They were so distant they might have come from another world. A third sounded.

"What was that?" Tim asked.

"Gunshots," Clint said.

"Keep going," said Rex. "They came from beyond them willows."

The horses had a difficult time picking up speed in the wet ground, but they did their best. A mile farther on, the four men cut through the willows and glimpsed a ranch in the distance. They realized the shots must have come from the ranch.

When they rode into the ranch's front yard, it was Tim who saw the horses first.

"Over there!" he said. "Look!"

Rex saw two horses cropping the grass under some trees behind the barn. One horse was saddled and the other was cruelly overloaded with leather sacks. Riding over swiftly, Rex and the others dismounted.

A quick inspection of the packhorse and the leather bags revealed the gold. But which of the two highwaymen's horses was the saddled one? Rex examined the stirrups. They were high. The horse belonged to the woman, he decided, which meant she was still in the ranch house and more than likely armed.

Her presence explained the shots they had heard.

"Sheriff!" a woman called.

Rex turned to see Annie Foster hurrying across the yard toward them. Though he knew the woman only from a distance, she appeared to know him well enough. Then this was Annie Foster's ranch; he had heard she still kept the place going in the valley.

"There's a woman in there who helped rob the stage, Sheriff!" Annie told him. "She's had a fearful blow on the head, but she's beginning to regain consciousness."

"This I want to see," Tim said, a smile on his face.

As the four men hurried across the yard with Annie, she explained who had fired the three shots they had heard and gave a graphic account of the violence and terror that had occurred shortly before and how Lone Bear had come to their rescue.

They had almost reached the ranch house when a woman came running out to greet John Ferris. The sheriff realized she must be Helen Bromfield. She obviously was overjoyed to see the actor, and from the look of her, Rex understood why Ferris had been so anxious to go after her.

They all crowded into the kitchen, and Rex saw Lorna May sitting in a kitchen chair, bound hand and foot. It appeared the kitchen table had been broken up, and its pieces were piled neatly in a corner. Annie Foster's two children were standing nervously beside the bound woman. While his younger sister clung to him, the towheaded boy was holding a cast-iron skillet in his hand, obviously meant to keep the groggy woman intimidated.

Lorna May turned her head at their approach. She appeared to be in some pain.

"You Lorna May?" Rex asked.

The woman nodded.

"And you helped rob the Cimarron stage?"

Again she nodded.

"You're under arrest. My deputy here will be bringing you back to Gunnison for trial. But you could help yourself some if you'd tell us where your partner was heading when he left here."

"How the hell would I know that? Does a scared rabbit know where it's goin'? Sutter's just runnin' now, Sheriff." She glanced uneasily at the towheaded boy standing beside her. "How about untying me? I'm afraid this kid is going to give me another slam on the head."

"It was I who did that," said Helen, stepping closer. There was a mean fire in her eyes. "I am only sorry it did not kill you."

The girl grinned crookedly at Helen. "Hell, maybe it did. I don't feel so good up there."

The statement seemed to sober Helen. She paled slightly and stepped back.

"Untie her," Rex said to Tim.

"Please excuse me," Annie said. "I must see to Lone Bear."

"I'd like to see him, too," the sheriff said.

They found the Indian lying on Annie Foster's bed. He was watching them alertly with large black eyes, his face pale, his upper torso bare. There was a hole in his side the size of a quarter. But the wound was clean, and Rex guessed that Annie Foster had been washing it out when they rode up.

"Annie told me how you got that wound," Rex said to the Indian. "We both figure you saved the boy's life coming in like that when you did."

"I should have come sooner. I ride too slow in the rain."

"Nonsense," Annie said. "You came when you could, and thank heaven you did. I shall never be able to thank you enough. That madman was going to fire on Ephraim."

"You're a Ute?" asked Rex.

The Indian nodded impassively, his eyes growing darker.

"Thought you were all down south of here, on a reservation near Animas Valley."

"Some of my people go. Some stay here—in the land of their fathers."

Rex considered that a moment, then smiled. "Well, sir, I'm sure glad you hung around. And I'll bet Annie is, too."

Touching his hat brim to the Indian in salute, he left the bedroom.

Annie hurried out after him anxiously. "Sheriff, Lone Bear's hurt bad. He keeps losing blood, and I don't know how to get that bullet out of him. Can you get help?"

"I'm going after Sutter. But when Tim takes the gold on to Cimarron, he could find a doctor. But that would take a good long time, and once word gets out there's a wounded Ute around here, the army might come looking. You wouldn't want that, ma'am, and I know Lone Bear wouldn't."

"You're not going to report his presence?" Annie asked.

"I am not."

She rested her hand gratefully on Rex's arm for a moment. "I'll do what I can by myself then," she said, and hurried back to the bedroom.

Less than an hour later Annie stood in her doorway with Ephraim and Marylou by her side, fighting back her tears. The sheriff and his party were pulling out, Rex to hunt down Carl Sutter and his deputy heading for Cimarron with the gold and Lorna May. Clint was riding along, and the sheriff had not yet decided what to do about him. Helen Bromfield and John Ferris were also accompanying them. Helen's long, terrible journey was nearly over.

Before she passed from sight, Helen turned in her saddle and waved to her new friends. Annie and the children waved back. Annie felt a terrible, empty loneliness as she did so. She found little comfort in Helen's promise to visit soon, for behind her in her bedroom, his life slowly draining away, was Lone Bear—and though she had tried valiantly, there seemed to be nothing she could do to help him. For the second time in her life, Annie knew utter despair.

Suddenly Ephraim raised his arm and pointed. "Look, Ma!"

Annie turned. An Indian rider was approaching from the south. As he got closer, Annie saw that he was a squat, older Ute with white hair.

"Stay here," she told her children. "I will greet him and see what he wants."

She walked out into the yard and waited for the Indian to pull up. He halted his pony and looked impassively down at her. "I am Running Fox," he said. "I bring medicine for Lone Bear."

Annie was astonished. How had this Indian found out about Lone Bear's terrible wound?

"Thank you for coming," she said eagerly. "Lone Bear is in my house. I will take you to him."

The Indian slid off his horse, lifted a very colorful medicine bag from his pony's neck, and followed Annie. Wide-eyed, Ephraim and Marylou watched the Indian march into the house behind their mother.

"Lone Bear is in there," Annie said, pointing to her bedroom.

The Indian nodded and went in. Annie cautioned Ephraim and Marylou with a finger to her lips, then followed after the medicine man. She saw Lone Bear's eyes light up the moment he glimpsed Running Fox. Almost at once, it seemed, color flowed back into his face. It was obvious that Lone Bear had great confidence in Running Fox's ability to help him.

Annie was enormously relieved. As she watched Running Fox inspect Lone Bear's wound, then swiftly open his bag and take out his salves and potions and a long, forcepslike bone instrument, she was certain that Lone Bear was going to survive. She could feel it in every fiber of her being. There was strength in him that no single bullet could extinguish.

In that instant, Annie realized that to be Lone Bear's squaw would be one thing, but to be his wife would be something else again.

Lone Bear looked up at Annie and smiled—and in that smile Annie saw all his love and trust. She went to the side of the bed and took one of his hands between hers. As they gazed into each other's eyes she knew they had silently come to an understanding, and she realized her eyes were misting over with happiness.

Chapter Eleven

The sun was poking brightly through the few remaining clouds when Rex saw Sutter's tracks drifting toward the river and told Tim, Clint, and the others to hold up. He followed Sutter's sign until he reached a narrow ford. The river was still rising. The sheriff knew he had better cross the river soon before it rose any higher. Beyond the river, on the far side of the valley, the peaks of the Bowie Range were no longer hidden by dark, swirling rain clouds. Rex realized that once Sutter crossed the mountains he would be difficult if not impossible to apprehend.

Rex wheeled his horse and rode back to his deputy. Leaving Lorna May in John Ferris's custody, the two lawmen found a place off the trail where they could talk without being overheard.

"I want you to continue on to Cimarron with Lorna May and the gold," Rex told Tim. "Dump her in the jail and take the gold to the express office. And while you're at it, I think maybe you better escort the gold out to the mines, as well."

159

"What about you, Rex?"

"I'm going after Sutter," the sheriff said.

"Alone?" Tim asked anxiously.

"I'm taking Clint with me."

Tim's jaw dropped open. "You want to explain that to me? I heard every word, but I don't think I understand."

Rex sliced a fresh chaw from his plug of tobacco and tossed it into his mouth.

"Sutter's already cut across the river," he explained patiently. "He's heading into the Bowie Range. I want to get him before he reaches it."

"But why in hell are you taking the bank robber?" Tim asked.

"Sutter will be ahead of me in the rocks. He'll have the advantage. Clint just might give me the edge I need."

"Dammit, Rex! That don't make no sense at all. What kind of an edge is a bank robber going to give you? We should've taken his gun long ago and searched his saddlebags. I'll bet you a hundred bucks the money is in there." The young deputy was clearly incensed at his boss's foolish idea.

"That's no bet. You're probably right."

"Then let me go with you, Rex. You know you can count on me," Tim pleaded.

"And who's going to take Lorna May in? And who's going to deliver that gold to Cimarron? Someone's got to go after Sutter and that someone's me. Besides, you know how much I want that sonofabitch. Look at it this way. I'm entrusting Lorna May and the gold to you. Clint will stay with me, and he'll be my responsibility," the sheriff explained.

"I don't like it, Rex."

"You don't have to like it. Just do it." Rex's voice was firm.

"If that's what you want," Tim said unhappily.

"That's what I want. Now go on back there and tell Clint I want to see him."

Tim nodded and hurried off to get Clint.

Two hours later, Clint and Rex were riding into the foothills of the Bowie Range.

When Rex had asked Clint to join him in going after Sutter, Clint had been more than a little wary. He was pretty sure that both the sheriff and his deputy knew it was he who had robbed the bank in Gunnison. Why they had not yet made a move to arrest him was a mystery, though Clint surmised it probably had to do with the complications brought about by the stage holdup. It had sure as hell made a mess of his own plans.

Once he reached Cimarron, Clint had planned to shake the sheriff and his deputy. He had not wanted to take on either man during the ride to Cimarron, not with John Ferris and Helen Bromfield as witnesses. Though he knew he should not allow it to influence him, he cared greatly what those two thought of him. But now that he was alone with the sheriff, Clint felt himself free to make his move. Not that it was going to be all that easy to surprise the old bloodhound riding alongside him.

They were moving into higher country, and twice Clint remarked on the pace Sutter was setting. The outlaw was obviously going flat out, if the tracks he was leaving were any indication. As they turned into a gravelly ravine, the sheriff reined in abruptly and dismounted.

"What is it, Sheriff?" Clint asked.

Rex studied Sutter's tracks, then squinted up at Clint. "Notice anything?"

"About those tracks?"

The sheriff nodded.

Clint dismounted and went down on one knee to peer more closely at the hoofprints Sutter's horse was leaving in the soft ground. Then he glanced up at the sheriff. "I don't see anything different. They seem pretty deep, though."

The sheriff smiled. "Any significance in that, do you think?"

Clint shrugged. "The ground's still soaked from the rain."

"Look at the tracks we're making," Rex suggested.

Clint straightened and walked back behind his mounts to study their tracks. The ground was still saturated, and they were probably no more than an hour behind Sutter, yet the tracks Clint and the sheriff were leaving were considerably lighter.

"There's a difference, all right," admitted Clint, rejoining the sheriff. "They don't go as deep as ours."

"And how would you account for that?"

"Sutter's mount is carrying something else beside Sutter. And that something is mighty heavy," Clint said.

The sheriff smiled. "And just what do you suppose that might be?"

"Gold."

Rex nodded. "The sonofabitch is still carrying gold. We didn't get it all back, it seems. Sutter left Annie's ranch in quite a hurry, according to Helen's account. Sutter must have been carrying the gold from the second packhorse when he rode up to the ranch, and it was still on his horse when he rode out."

Clint frowned thoughtfully. "That means Sutter's horse won't last. Not at the rate he's pushing it. And not if his mount has to lug that gold, too."

The sheriff agreed emphatically. "That's how I figure it. Sutter is going to lose his mount just the way he lost that packhorse before."

Clint recalled John Ferris's words. They were singularly apt. "Sutter's a fool, sure enough," Clint mused. "A man without any imagination."

"What's that?" Rex asked.

"Just thinking out loud, Sheriff."

With a curt nod, the sheriff swung back up onto his horse. Clint mounted up as well, and the two men rode on into the ravine. Soon the walls closed in and the bright sky overhead shrank. As they rode, both men kept their eyes on the rocks above them. If Sutter had thought of doubling back and bushwhacking anyone on his tail, this would be an excellent place for it.

But half a mile farther on they emerged from the ravine onto a sunlit park without incident. The ground held a light cover of sparse, burned-out pasture grass and a few weeds that had already gone to seed. Despite the recent rain the surface was well drained for the most part. The hoofprints left by Sutter's horse no longer sank so deeply into the turf, but from the length of the animal's stride, Sutter was still pushing his mount hard.

A stream appeared off to their right, tumbling swiftly through the cleft in a stretch of cap rock. The sheriff swung his mount in that direction.

"We'd best water the horses," he said. "And rest them up some, too."

Clint agreed.

As the two dismounted and lifted the saddles off their mounts, the sheriff glanced at Clint, one eyebrow cocked.

"Did you notice Sutter's tracks?"

Clint smiled. "Sure."

"They went right on past this stream. Sutter sure as hell is doing his best to run that horse of his into the ground," Rex said.

"I noticed." Clint nodded.

"Sutter's got no imagination. Right?"

Clint was startled. Grinning suddenly, he nodded. "That's what I figure, Sheriff."

"It'll get him caught."

"Or worse," Clint suggested.

The two men watered their horses, then set them loose to graze for a while. Clint lay back full length on the cap rock, his face to the sky, his arms folded under his head, and did his best to quiet his nerves. But whenever he thought of the inevitable moment somewhere ahead when he would have to draw on the sheriff, he got sick inside. It was not fear he felt. It was something a lot more difficult to deal with. He liked and respected the sheriff too much to turn on him. It sure as hell was not easy to be an outlaw, Clint decided.

Not long after resuming the trail, as they were crossing a flat area below a ridge, they both caught sight of a rider cresting the ridge about a mile ahead of them. As horse and rider stood out sharply for a moment, the rider turned in his saddle. Sunlight glinted on metal. Then he was gone.

"You think he saw us?" asked Clint.

"He saw us, all right."

"That means he'll be waiting for us up ahead somewhere," Clint pointed out.

"That's what it means. You want to turn back?" Rex asked.

"I was just commenting, Sheriff. No need to get your back up," Clint said.

Later that afternoon, Rex suddenly pulled up and dismounted. They were a mile into a steep, winding canyon littered with boulders, some of which were as big as houses. As Clint watched without dismounting, the sheriff disappeared into a stand of scrub pine growing close to the base of the cliff.

He reappeared a moment later and waved Clint closer. Dismounting, Clint pushed through the pine and found the sheriff standing before a large flat boulder lodged flush against the canyon wall. The ground around the boulder was beaten down by footprints.

"There's a tree branch over there," the sheriff told Clint, pointing to a gully about ten feet farther on. "We'll need it to pry up this boulder."

Clint fetched the branch.

"Looks like it's already been used," he said to the sheriff, as he tapped some fresh scratches on one end of the branch.

"And most likely for the same purpose."

Together, they thrust the bruised end of the branch under the boulder and lifted. At once both of them glimpsed some leather bags tucked securely into a hollowed-out depression beneath the boulder.

"I'll hold this steady while you pull them out," Clint said.

"No need to do that yet," said the sheriff. "It won't go anywhere. We'll pick it up on our way back."

"Maybe you better check to make sure the gold's in there," Clint suggested.

The sheriff shrugged, reached in under the boulder, and pulled one of the bags out. Opening it swiftly, he pulled out a sack of gold coins.

Clint nodded.

The sheriff shoved the bag back in under the boulder, then helped Clint lower the boulder onto the gold. As Rex was lowering the boulder, Clint noticed the man's color—deathly white. The air so high in the mountains was light, chill even, and neither man had exerted himself very much. Yet tiny beads of perspiration were standing out on the sheriff's forehead.

Suddenly Clint knew why.

The moment the sheriff reached in under that boulder, he had been waiting for Clint to let it fall on him. Though it had not occurred to Clint to do such a thing, there was no way the sheriff could have known that. But he had gone ahead anyway, gambling his life on Clint's integrity.

"Sutter's getting smart, looks like," Clint said to the sheriff as they started back to their horses. "He's lightening his mount."

"It's too late."

"Why do you say that?" Clint asked.

"When a man like Sutter notices his animal laboring, it's already too late," Rex replied.

"His mount's just about gone, then."

Rex smiled. "That's what I think."

Swinging up into his saddle, Clint peered at the trail ahead of him. It was winding and treacherous, with any number of vantage points from which to fire down on them. Carl Sutter had already killed at least two men. He might be stupid when it came to horses, but there was no evidence that this failing in any way hampered his aim.

The sheriff remounted and glanced back at Clint. "I'll go ahead. You keep back. No sense in giving that sonofabitch two good targets at the same time."

"You figure he's close by?"

"We'll find his dead horse first. It'll be up here not too far ahead of us, I'm thinking."

They both spotted the dead horse at the same time. It was on the trail ahead of them, about two hundred yards distant. Barely visible at first, it reminded Clint of a woman's oversized purse gleaming in the sun. Glancing up, Clint saw two buzzards hanging in the sky high above the cliffs.

They had almost reached the dead horse when the sheriff turned in his saddle and warned, "Keep an eye out!"

A second later Clint heard the sharp crack of a rifle, its shattering roar racing through the canyon. As the bullet whined off a rock beside him, the sheriff grabbed his rifle and hurled himself from his saddle, making for a huge boulder beside the trail. A second later Clint pulled up behind the same boulder, carrying his own rifle.

"Try to draw his fire," said the sheriff. "I want to see where the sonofabitch is."

"I'll make for that rise near the cliff face," Clint told him.

The sheriff nodded and poked his head up carefully. "Now!" he said.

Clint ran out from behind the boulder, and digging hard, scrambled up the steep embankment, heading for the clump of scrub pine at its crest. He was halfway up the slope when Sutter began firing at him. He was good, Clint had to admit, as Sutter's rapid fire sent geysers of sand and stone into the air all about him. But he was not quite good enough.

Clint reached the crest of the rise unscathed and ducked into the pines. Flattening himself behind a boulder, he looked back through the pines to where the sheriff was crouching.

"Come ahead!" Clint shouted.

The sheriff moved fast for a man near fifty. And again Sutter was good, but not good enough. Breathing heavily, the sheriff flopped down beside Clint.

"He's right over us on a ledge that commands this whole damn canyon," the sheriff told Clint bitterly. "He might even have shot that horse and left it there to draw us all the way in. I wouldn't put it past him."

"You're giving him too much credit," Clint said.

"Maybe."

"How are we going to work this?" Clint asked.

"I say we split up, come at the ledge from two angles. Get above him if we can," Rex suggested.

"Show me the ledge."

The sheriff pointed it out to Clint. It was an eagle's nest high above the canyon floor, with an unobstructed view of the slope below. Clint studied the steep canyon wall for a moment, then found what he was looking for farther down.

"There's a game trail over there," he told the sheriff, pointing. "It'll take me high enough to make that cleft in the rock face. From there, I should have no trouble getting above him."

"Yeah, I see it. I'll cover you until you reach the trail. Then I'll make for the rocks farther down. Looks like it'll take me a while to get above him, but that slope isn't so steep."

"You think you can get above him from there?" Clint wondered.

The sheriff looked at him. "If I can't, you should be able to. All right, go ahead. I'll cover you. When you get set, cover me."

Clint braced himself, got a firm grip on his rifle, then burst from the pines, heading for the cliff wall. He had not taken two steps before Sutter opened up, the bullets whining uncomfortably close. From behind him came the sheriff's rapid volley. Sutter's fire slowly diminished, then stopped entirely. A moment later, Clint reached the game trail and began scrambling up the slope. It had looked negotiable enough from the pines. But moving across the steep cliff wall, he realized he had a difficult climb ahead of him.

Once he was high enough, he crouched behind a cleft in the rock face and opened up on Sutter's ledge, firing carefully, steadily, his intention simply to keep Sutter's head down.

Glancing at the pines below, he saw the sheriff make his move. The big man was quick, and Sutter only got off two or three futile rounds before the sheriff ducked safely among the rocks on the other side of the ledge. Clint left the cleft and continued to climb.

He was coming out just above the ledge when he had a thought—a very unpleasant one. Why the hell should Sutter have waited on the ledge after he saw both of them start up after him? Surely he must know what Clint and the sheriff's intentions were.

The thought pulled Clint up short. Ducking down, he took the opportunity to get his breath and study the situation a little more closely. He was coming out onto a narrow finger of rock that would take him to within twenty feet of the ledge just below him. There, supposedly, Carl Sutter would be squatting, his eyes on the canyon below.

Glancing almost straight up, Clint caught sight of a beetling crown of rock at the very rim of the canyon and high enough to command the entire slope—and anyone on it. Clint spun around and moved back the way he had come.

When he had gone about twenty feet, he took off his boots and then his socks. Dropping his spurs and socks into his boots, he cached them behind a rock. The sun was still high enough to keep the rocks hot, and Clint found himself moving faster than he wanted as he clambered up the exposed rock faces barefoot, heading for the rocky brow he had sighted from below. His bare feet gave him a sure grip on the smooth rock.

Reaching the rock overhang, he flung himself face down and looked over. Less than ten feet below him Carl Sutter was crouched on the crown of a boulder. Below Sutter the sheriff was moving into plain sight on a narrow trail. He was just above the ledge where Sutter had positioned himself earlier.

As Clint watched, Sutter reached for his rifle. The sheriff obviously had no idea Sutter was above him. And in a moment, if Sutter's aim was adequate, Sheriff Rex Barney would be a dead man.

In that instant it occurred to Clint that here was the answer to all his problems. He could let Sutter kill the sheriff, then shoot down Sutter. There was gold cached back on the trail that only he would know about. And Clint's father would have the money he needed to save his ranch. All Clint had to do was keep his mouth shut and hold his fire.

"Freeze, Sutter!" Clint barked. "Fire that rifle and you're a dead man!"

Sutter's reaction astonished Clint. Cursing violently, he spun and fired up at Clint, levered swiftly, then fired again. He was in a fury and continued to send a murderous barrage up at Clint. Like angry hornets, the slugs ricocheted off the ledge. Caught by surprise, Clint pushed himself back and kept his head down until he heard the sheriff open up on Sutter from below. As soon as Sutter's fire slowed, Clint cautiously peered over the ledge. Sutter was down on one knee, a bright streak of blood snaking down the rock face from underneath him.

"Drop the rifle!" Clint yelled. "Now!"

Instead, Sutter spun and aimed his rifle. This time Clint was ready. He fired, levered, and fired again. Two puffs of dust erupted from Sutter's vest. Sutter's rifle clattered to the ground as the two slugs flung him backward. Like a child's rag doll, Sutter tumbled backward off the rock. As he fell, his lifeless body bounced off two ledges, then vanished into a tangle of rocks far below on the canyon floor.

Emerging from behind a boulder, Sheriff Rex Barney looked up at Clint and waved. Clint waved back, then glanced up at the sky. Another vulture had already joined the first two.

Chapter Twelve

"**H**e don't look like much, and that's a fact," said the sheriff, gazing down at Sutter's broken body.

"Neither did the stage driver and that shotgun rider."

The sheriff glanced at him. "It was you that buried them under that cairn, wasn't it?"

"John Ferris and me. We didn't have any shovels. And we didn't want to leave them to the buzzards."

"I knew MacDougal and Billy. Liked them both. Thanks," Rex said sincerely.

"About this fellow here. You think we ought to bother covering what's left of him?" Clint asked.

"No, I don't." The sheriff glanced up at the sky. It was filling up fast with black wings.

Clint nodded and walked over to his horse. As he was adjusting his cinch a moment later, the sheriff stopped beside him.

"I'll need some help lifting up that boulder, and I figure all that gold would be too much for my horse to carry alone. He's about done in. Thought maybe we might split the load between us,'' he suggested.

"Sure," Clint agreed.

"Thanks."

"Not at all, Sheriff. Glad to oblige."

The sheriff paused. Clint could tell the man wanted to say something—something important. But he could not get it out.

Clint swung up into his saddle and smiled down at the sheriff. "You don't need to thank me for drawing that louse's fire when I did," he said. "I was as surprised to find him on that rock below me as you were to find him above you."

"Clint, if you hadn't drawn down on him when you did . . ." Rex's voice trailed away.

"Guess you're just lucky, Sheriff. Hell, we both are. Let's go get that gold and head on into Cimarron. I'm thinking maybe I'd like to sleep between sheets tonight."

The sheriff smiled wearily. "Yeah. Guess I would, too."

When they rode into Cimarron a little after dusk, Rex turned his horse toward the express office and pulled up in front of it. Dismounting, he climbed the steps and entered the office.

When the astonished clerk saw Rex, he put down his pen and shoved his green eyeshade back off his forehead.

Rex nodded to him. "Howdy, Fred."

"Where'd you drop from, Sheriff? Tim said you went after Carl Sutter."

"That's right, I did."

The clerk tried to peer past the sheriff at the hitch rail. "Did you bring him in?"

"Nope. Left him where he fell. Has Tim taken that gold to the mine yet?"

"You just missed him," the clerk said.

"Well, I got some more gold. Open up that safe, will you?" Rex asked.

"Did you say gold, Sheriff?"

"You heard right."

Rex left the office and descended the porch steps. Clint was standing beside his mount, untying the leather sacks from his saddle horn. Rex removed the saddlebags he used to carry his share of the gold, then followed Clint up the steps into the office. The clerk was hastily pulling open the safe. Clint and Rex both dropped their bags on the floor.

"That it, Sheriff?" the clerk asked, his eyes wide.

"That's all we got. I'd appreciate an accurate count as soon as you can get it to me. I'll be at the hotel."

"Sure thing, Sheriff."

Rex knew the clerk was almost beside himself with curiosity, but he had no intention of telling him anything more. He nodded to Clint, and both men left the office.

They mounted up and headed for the livery stable, where they left their horses. Afterward they crossed the narrow street with their gear and entered the hotel. While signing the register, Rex turned to his companion. "Would you join me for dinner, Clint?" he asked.

Clint hesitated for a moment, then shrugged. "Sure. Just let me stow my gear first."

"I'll wait for you in the hotel restaurant, then. Take your time—as much as you need. I'll be wetting my whistle at the bar."

With a curt nod, Rex turned and walked into the hotel bar. He did not look back. And he did not expect to see Clint again. Rex had already decided he would give Clint two hours to shake Cimarron's dust, maybe even three. At least until Tim got back. Then Rex would have to go after Clint. He did not want to, but he had no choice. The best he could do was give Clint a good start.

Rex owed him that much at least.

Clint watched the sheriff disappear into the bar. He understood perfectly what Rex's intentions were. During the ride to Cimarron, the sheriff had been obviously troubled. He was wrestling with a man-sized dilemma, and this was his solution.

Because Rex felt he owed Clint, he was giving Clint a chance to light out. And there was a good chance that if Clint took this chance the sheriff was giving him, by the next morning Clint would be at his father's ranch, ready to climb onto a fresh mount. He just might make it, after all.

Pulling his saddlebags off the front desk, Clint turned and hurried out of the hotel. When he reached the livery stable, he asked the hostler if he had watered and grained his mount yet.

"You just brought him in," the old man drawled, sending a powerful shot of tobacco juice from the corner of his mouth. "What's your hurry?"

"Never mind. I'll buy a fresh mount. What've you got you can let me have?"

The old codger's eyes lit up. "Well, now, it just so happens I have just the horse for a man as big and lank as you. A big, powerful black, never ridden hard. Colonel Potter—he lives just out of town—was too old to give this animal a proper workout, so he's a mite frisky. But he's got the legs and the heart."

"Let me see him," Clint requested.

The black looked healthy enough, but even as Clint checked its mouth and then ran his hand down its powerful

176

flanks, he knew he was not going to purchase the horse and ride out of Cimarron. Not that night, anyway. He had a dinner engagement with Sheriff Rex Barney.

He stepped out of the stall. "A fine animal," he said to the hostler, "but I think I'll wait awhile before I switch mounts."

He flipped a quarter to the old man for his trouble and walked from the livery stable. A moment later, still carrying his saddlebags, he strode into the hotel saloon and sidled up to the bar beside the sheriff.

The sheriff almost dropped the glass he was holding.

"Why don't we go into the restaurant and find a table, Sheriff?" Clint said. "I'm as hungry as a bear. Bring your drink."

After they had given the waiter their order, Clint decided it was time to introduce himself. "Sheriff, my full name's Clint Dennison."

The sheriff nodded. He was still too astonished at Clint's return to say anything.

"And I have something for you," Clint said, pushing his saddlebag across the table to the sheriff.

The sheriff swallowed as he reached out for the saddlebag. "Is this what I think it is?"

"I reckon so."

"Why, Clint? Dammit! You know what I meant back there in the lobby. I was giving you a chance to light out," Rex said.

"You don't owe me, Sheriff, and I got enough imagination to know I can't run from you forever. I'd sooner try to outrun an Apache. Besides, if it ever came to a showdown between us, you know damn well I couldn't pull the trigger."

"Hell, Clint, neither could I," the sheriff said with a smile.

Clint grinned. "So there's the money I borrowed. All of it."

Taking a deep breath, the sheriff opened the saddlebag's flap, reached in and pulled out the bills. He began counting.

Clint leaned back and waited. He felt enormously relieved, but saddened, too. He did not want his father to lose his ranch, but it looked like he was going to. Clint had done all he could to prevent that—more than his father would have wanted—but that gave him little comfort.

The sheriff finished counting and looked up, an anxious frown on his face.

"What's wrong, Sheriff?"

"Clint, where's the other sixteen thousand?" Rex asked.

"How much have you had to drink, Sheriff? I needed four thousand dollars, so that's what I took. I left an IOU with your bank president, but he didn't seem to think it was worth much. But like I told him, I would have paid it back—all of it," Clint said and handed the sheriff his father's letter.

The sheriff read it swiftly, then handed it back to Clint. "All right," Rex said. "Just let me get this straight. Your father needs four thousand to save his ranch. So you took that amount from the Miner's and Cattleman's Savings and Loan. No more. No less. And you left an IOU with Merlin Oppenheimer."

Clint nodded. "If Merlin Oppenheimer's the bank president, yes."

All at once a crafty light sprang into the sheriff's eyes. Suddenly he leaned forward. "Clint, there's two men involved in this here bank robbery—and one of them is the bank president!''

''What in the blazes do you mean, Sheriff?''

''Merlin Oppenheimer says you took twenty thousand. You didn't. But twenty thousand is missing. So guess who has the other sixteen?'' Rex asked.

''Oppenheimer!'' Clint could not believe what the man had done.

The sheriff nodded, his face grim. ''That crafty old miser! He saw his chance to line his pockets and took it!''

''What do we do now?''

''I want you to come back to Gunnison with me and confront the old sonofabitch,'' Rex said. ''It's a cinch Oppenheimer won't prosecute—not unless he wants to stand trial alongside you. Besides, all any of us in Gunnison want is that money back in the bank's vaults—and Oppenheimer put on notice that from now on he must be a very honest man.''

''Suppose he's already left with the sixteen thousand?'' Clint suggested.

''I doubt it. It would be a dead giveaway if he up and left town a few days after his bank was robbed. No. He's biding his time, counting on you being long gone—and me coming back empty-handed. And he won't know any different until we ride in.'' Rex smiled at the thought of the look on the banker's face when he walked in with Clint.

''Sheriff, I'd like to visit my father before I ride back to Gunnison. His ranch is only a day's ride from here. I won't have the money he needs, but maybe I can give him some comfort.''

''I'd like to go with you, Clint, and meet your father. Maybe I can help some with that comfort. I have a sneaking suspicion that Merlin Oppenheimer is going to be more than willing to cooperate with you and your father—financially, that is—in return for your silence and mine.''

Clint leaned back in his chair, dazed. Then he would be getting that loan for his father, after all. There would be all the collateral the fool bank president asked for, only this time it would not be coming from the barrel of a Colt .45.

Helen was on the porch of her new schoolhouse when she glanced up and saw Sheriff Rex Barney and Clint Dennison riding toward them on their way out of town. She hurried back inside the schoolhouse.

''John!'' she called. ''Come quickly.''

John Ferris looked up from inspecting one of the children's desks.

''What is it, Helen?''

''The sheriff and Clint are riding by! Come say hello!'' Helen urged.

Ferris hurried down the aisle and stepped out onto the porch with Helen. They both waved and shouted to the two riders, who stopped, then turned their horses to the schoolhouse. Helen and Ferris descended the stairs to meet the two men as they pulled up.

''I see you made it all right,'' the sheriff said, smiling down at Helen.

''Yes, thanks to you—and so many others,'' she replied. ''It's a fine school. Everything is brand new, and I've already met some of my new pupils. They seem so anxious for school to begin.''

''I told her she shouldn't count on that lasting for long,'' Ferris said, laughing.

''You two look very happy,'' Clint commented.

Helen felt herself blush. Ferris smiled proudly.

"Helen and I will be getting married come this fall," he told Clint, "and I'll be her teaching partner here. I'll teach the upper grades, she'll teach the primary. English literature and poetry will be my specialties. And who knows, maybe I'll put on a few plays now and then and do a reading if the occasion is right."

"And of course you're both invited to the wedding," Helen said. "I hope you can come."

"We'll be there," the sheriff promised.

"Sounds like it should be a fine match," Clint said. "Congratulations to you both."

Ferris shook his head in wonder. "It's strange, Clint. Before you and I joined forces to go after Sutter, I was ready to give up. I was convinced the final curtain was on its way down for me." He chuckled ruefully. "I was even developing a cough to prove it. But since that night you and I spent huddled in the rain—me talking my fool head off—I haven't coughed once. And all I want to do now is live."

Helen moved closer to Ferris and took his arm.

"I'm glad everything worked out for you, actor," Clint said warmly. "You ride a horse well and made a fine companion—after you stopped shooting at snakes, that is."

Ferris grinned, and Helen wondered what Clint was talking about. She decided she would make Ferris tell her as soon as she got the chance.

"Sheriff," she said, "everyone in Cimarron is talking about you! I heard you rode into the express office last evening with the rest of the gold. I also heard that Carl Sutter is dead. Is that correct?"

"Right both times."

Helen shuddered slightly. "He was such a horrid

man, yet I don't feel any pleasure at the thought of his death."

"That's only Christian, ma'am. But he was a mean one, all right. He almost killed me. If it weren't for Clint here, I'd be getting fitted for a halo, or a pitchfork, about now."

Ferris stepped closer. "What about Lorna May?" he asked.

"Soon's I get back, she'll be taking the stage to Gunnison with my deputy—the next sheriff of Gunnison County," Rex said.

"You mean you're quitting?" Helen asked.

The sheriff nodded. "I'm getting me a little horse ranch in the hills north of Gunnison. You two be sure and come visit when you get settled."

"John and I will certainly do that," Helen assured him eagerly. "And where are you both off to now?"

"After supper last night, Clint and I painted the town a broad shade of red," the sheriff drawled. "We figure a long ride in the open air would be just the thing to clear our heads. Clint's father has a ranch not far from here, and we're going to give him a visit." He glanced at Clint. "You feeling any better, ol' buddy?"

"Some," Clint said with a grin. "But we'd best keep riding."

"Yeah," said the sheriff. "It's a fine morning and looks like it'll be an even better day."

The sheriff waved good-bye and Clint touched the brim of his hat to Helen, as the two men swung their horses about and rode away. Helen climbed the porch steps with John Ferris and watched them go.

She was thinking of what Ferris had told Clint and realized how much of it was true for her, as well. She, too, had changed, in almost every way. She had stepped onto that Cimarron stage certain of only one thing—that she hated all men. But the two riding out—and certainly the man standing close beside her—had taught her how foolish such a blanket condemnation could be.

As Clint and Rex vanished into the bright morning, Helen smiled. They were obviously such good friends. She wished them well.

Coming in November 1984 . . .

FROM THE
CREATORS OF WAGONS WEST

STAGECOACH

STATION 15:

WICHITA

HANK MITCHUM

In September 1871, a stagecoach rolls into Wichita, Kansas, bearing a man with a past that he hopes to put behind him—the famous gunfighter Layne Britton. He has come to lay claim to a ranch left him by his deceased uncle. It is in Wichita that he meets the stunning Connie Lee, who is mourning the recent death of her mother.

Also in Wichita is Connie's stepfather, Dolph Catron, an unscrupulous lawyer who will stop at nothing to win control over the city. He has long had his eye on the land owned by Layne's uncle, and when the famous gunman arrives in town, Catron hatches a plan to get rid of Layne and secure the land for himself. He will let nothing and no one stand in his way—not even Connie Lee.

As events thunder toward the final showdown, with Layne imprisoned after being framed for a murder he did not commit and with Connie's own life hanging in the balance, Connie must come to terms with her true feelings for both Layne and her real father—a man who himself once fell victim to the evil machinations of Dolph Catron.

Read WICHITA, on sale November 15, 1984, wherever Bantam paperbacks are sold.

★ WAGONS WEST ★

A series of unforgettable books that trace the lives of a dauntless band of pioneering men, women, and children as they brave the hazards of an untamed land in their trek across America. This legendary caravan of people forge a new link in the wilderness. They are Americans from the North and the South, alongside immigrants, Blacks, and Indians, who wage fierce daily battles for survival on this uncompromising journey—each to their private destinies as they fulfill their greatest dreams.

☐	24408	INDEPENDENCE!	$3.95
☐	24651	NEBRASKA!	$3.95
☐	24229	WYOMING!	$3.95
☐	24088	OREGON!	$3.95
☐	23168	TEXAS!	$3.50
☐	24655	CALIFORNIA!	$3.95
☐	24694	COLORADO!	$3.95
☐	20174	NEVADA!	$3.50
☐	20919	WASHINGTON!	$3.50
☐	22925	MONTANA!	$3.95
☐	23572	DAKOTA!	$3.95
☐	23921	UTAH!	$3.95
☐	24256	IDAHO!	$3.95

Prices and availability subject to change without notice.

Buy them at your local bookstore or use this handy coupon: